"A winner. The characters feel real, the dialogue is killer bee, and, for better or worse, the book smells like New York. Possibly more important, the book satisfies Raymond Chandler's famous criterion for all good fiction: 'it creates the illusion of life.' While Bogart's prose is smart, funny and up-to-date, at times it seems to also attain a grainy, almost ruthless quality, redolent of another era. There is a soul-searching simplicity about this author's style that combines with possibly rarer, harder-to-trace elements to make this mystery novel more than a mystery novel. . . . *PLAY IT AGAIN* offers the reader what every good mystery novel should—a sense of resolution that, unfortunately, life itself rarely provides. . . . [Bogart's] talent, toughness, and charm, however, are uniquely his own, and they should shine brightly in the pale critical light of what we call modern fiction."

—*Washington Post Book World*

"While the magic name Bogart assures *PLAY IT AGAIN* a place on any list of bestsellers, Stephen Bogart's prose stands on its own. Sharp, funny, self-deprecating, and scrupulously honest from the crown of his fedora to the soles of his gum shoes, R.J. Brooks is a detective for our and any other time. To read this book for the first time is to know the thrill of discovering a previously unreleased film starring You-Know-Who."

—Loren D. Estleman

"R.J. Brooks has a heavy family history of Hollywood fame. To R.J., his mother's career was a curse, but when she is murdered he becomes Nemesis. Suspenseful and tight. I hope Bogart plans an R.J. Brooks series. Here's looking at you, kid."

—Barbara D'Amato, author of the *Cat Marsala* novels

PLAY IT AGAIN

STEPHEN HUMPHREY
BOGART

A TOM DOHERTY ASSOCIATES BOOK
NEW YORK

This is a work of fiction. All the characters and events portrayed in this book are fictitious, and any resemblance to real people or events is purely coincidental.

PLAY IT AGAIN

Cover art by Richard Andri

A Forge Book
Published by Tom Doherty Associates, Inc.
175 Fifth Avenue
New York, N.Y. 10010

Forge® is a registered trademark of Tom Doherty Associates, Inc.

ISBN: 0-812-55162-1
Library of Congress Card Catalog Number: 94-44452

First edition: April 1995
First mass market edition: June 1996

Printed in the United States of America

0 9 8 7 6 5 4 3 2 1

To Barbara, for her love and support—
and
To my children, without whom there would be no R.J.
Brooks

CHAPTER 1

There was a bullet hole in his windshield, courtesy of a Tong hothead down in Chinatown, just so nobody forgot he was in a serious trade. His business card read:

R. J. Brooks
Matrimonial Detective

It was the lowest form of sleuthing. His clients—mostly bluestocking lawyers from Manhattan law firms—generally used slimeball types for this kind of work, but R.J. had a reputation. He was reliable and effective.

R.J. didn't look like a sleazy private eye, and that was a professional plus. He knew his way around the upper and lower East Sides, and he could mix with the cream as well as the curd. He was fiercely loyal to his clients, even if he detested their sordid lifestyles. He never betrayed a confidentiality to the police, a judge, a journalist, or anyone else, and he never padded his expense accounts.

In fact, in a lot of ways he was an average guy. For starters, like a lot of other guys, he had trouble with his mother.

His mother had aged. They all did, but to her it was more of a tragedy. And since she figured she might have missed out on telling him a few things the first time around, she tried to make up for it now. That doesn't sit so well with a guy in his thirties, in a tough profession.

The problem was worse because she was right: She *had* missed out on a hell of a lot of stuff when he was a kid. In fact, he had been raised pretty much without her. Of course she'd been busy, he didn't argue that.

It was a full-time job being a movie star.

And even now, at her age, it was still a full-time job. Which was one reason he hated being seen in public with her. Her friends were bad enough. But to see normal, rational people falling all over themselves at the sight of his mother—it was enough to gag an alley cat.

Still, she was his mother. He saw her only once or twice a year. So when she called with one of her "Darling I'm in town for just a day or two" invitations to lunch, he tried to do the right thing and see her.

Unless, of course, he could come up with a really good excuse.

But this time he'd come up blank. Probably because he'd let his brain go soft the last week or so. He had just finished a lucrative but remarkably vile divorce case, and he was feeling burned out. But he could afford to be, for a week or two. He was way ahead for a change, bucks in the bank. He hadn't taken on anything new yet. He was just relaxing, enjoying himself in the greatest city in the world.

He'd taken in a couple of ballgames, gone to the track, even let a woman he was seeing drag him downtown to some dismal theater built around a grease pit in a converted garage. They'd seen something that probably didn't sound as pompous in German, but in English it was tough to take. The woman had made it up to him by taking him to the opera later that week, and that had been a good one, one R.J. could sing along to.

It was a good week. It wasn't often R.J. could afford to let himself drift, and he was enjoying the hell out of it, with no thought about getting back to work.

He should have known it wouldn't last.

Just as he was starting to think that life was a good thing for a change, the phone call had come.

"Darling," she said. She always said that. Couldn't bring herself to say "hello" like a normal person, because there was nothing normal about Belle Fontaine.

"Oh. Hello, Mom."

The long hiss of cigarette smoke blowing out of her lungs. "Well, don't overwhelm me with filial affection, R.J."

"It's a little late to worry about that, isn't it?"

More smoke. "All right, R.J. Forget I said anything."

"Sure thing. So how's tricks in the screen trade?"

"Actually, darling, I'm just in town for a couple of days about another Broadway thing. I thought we could have lunch."

Oh, Christ, he thought, but what he said was, "I'm kind of busy today, Mom."

"Perfect, darling, so am I. Shall we say tomorrow, one o'clock?"

You stepped in it now, sport, he said to himself. "Russian Tea Room again?"

"Of course, dear, it's a lovely place."

"It's a tacky place. Nobody hangs out there but old queens and wannabees."

"Really? And which am I, dear? An old wannabee?"

"For Christ's sake, Mom."

"Because I hang out there, dear, and I happen to like it there," she said, and R.J. could hear her lighting another cigarette.

"All right," he said. "It's Heaven on earth. The food is marvelous, the company divine, and the ambience is devastatingly witty, carefree, and bohemian. Now get off my case, okay?"

"My God, you remind me of your father," she said. "You even *sound* like him when you get mean."

"I'll see you at one o'clock tomorrow," R.J. said and hung up, suddenly weary of the game. They always ended up saying the same cruel things, and it always hurt.

R.J. spent the rest of the day walking downtown and snarling at strangers. He thought about seeing a movie but couldn't find one worth the price of the ticket.

He thought about going to a bar and watching a ballgame on TV, but he had been sober too long to want to hang out in a bar.

So R.J. had a hot dog in Times Square and took the subway home. One last big night on the town.

The next day he was at the Russian Tea Room, near Central Park, about ten minutes late. He was still there ahead of his mother. He stood for another twenty minutes with the maitre d' looking at him the way he'd look at a turd in a finger bowl.

He knew from the adrenaline-soaked murmuring that suddenly sprang up all around him, and he didn't have to turn to look at the door, but he did anyway. Everybody did.

Belle Fontaine had arrived.

An admiring throng pressed in on Belle and an elfin companion, but she plowed through without even seeing them. Straight for the maitre d'. The maitre d' had seen it all, had turned away more celebrities than William Morris, but even he was impressed. His whole face was one big, unctuous smile.

For somebody who hadn't worked more than a few weeks in fifteen years, Belle still commanded a tremendous amount of interest. "It's the legs," she would always say, but R.J. knew she was wrong.

The truth was, she had It, whatever It was. She could walk into a room filled with celebrities, athletes, politicians, whatever. And everybody would stop breathing and look at her.

Which was exactly what was happening now.

Here we go, thought R.J. Belle paraded up and planted a kiss on his cheek. He returned it dutifully.

She put her hands on his shoulders and stepped back, looking him over. "You look terrible," she announced.

"Thanks," he said. "You look swell."

"You need to lose a little weight. Exercise. Do you even take the vitamins I send you?"

"No," he said. "Let's eat something, all right? We can tear each other to shreds much better with something in our stomachs."

R.J. turned to where the fawning maitre d' was stuck in a half bow, pointing the way toward a table. "Keep that up, you're gonna need a chiropractor, Jack," he said.

Behind him his mother snorted and the elf snickered.

They worked their way through the room to a table in front, where Belle was properly displayed. She was on good behavior and only stopped to schmooze twice.

R.J. finally got a seat under him and sank into it

gratefully. He watched the waiter and the elf go through the ceremonial seating of Belle. So did everybody else in the place.

"You're supposed to wait until the lady is seated, R.J.," his mother said as she finally pulled her chair in to the table.

"I might faint from fatigue if I had to wait for you," he said.

She shook her head. "You always have to have a smart answer."

He bared his front teeth in a parody of a smile. "I'm a smart guy," he said.

She lit a cigarette, looked him over. He could see her decide to start again. "This is Michael, R.J.," she said, indicating the elf. "He's the most wonderful musical lyricist on Broadway."

"How do you *do,*" Michael said. "I've heard *so* much about you."

"That's good news," said R.J.

"Michael has been working on a few numbers for a backer's audition," Belle said. "We plan to have something ready for Christmas."

"After *all,*" gushed Michael, "she was so wonderful in the last show, it's just a *shame* not to get her right back on the *boards* again."

It was always the same, thought R.J. Belle was always looking for a comeback, and there was always some sleazy little weasel ready to ride her attempt into his fifteen minutes of fame. It made him tired, and a little sad, to see his mother drag herself through these demeaning gyrations.

"Why can't you let it go?" R.J. said. "You could afford to retire, you know."

She looked daggers at him. "My career is important to me, R.J. And plenty of people still know who I am."

"Sure they do," said R.J. "Why wouldn't they? You spend enough on your publicist."

"Must you be so cruel, R.J.?"

"I guess not," he said wearily. "How about you?"

She stubbed out her cigarette. "Michael, go make a phone call."

Michael hesitated just a second, and Belle swung her incredible blue eyes at him. He popped up instantly, sweat beading on his upper lip, and slithered away to the back of the restaurant.

"What rock did you find him under?" R.J. asked her.

"He's a very clever lyricist," she said defensively.

"I got a pal who's very clever at leg-breaking," R.J. said. "But I didn't bring him to lunch."

"All right, R.J., I'm sorry. I shouldn't have brought Michael along, and I know it. I just couldn't face you alone."

R.J. nodded. "You never could," he said quietly.

"But can't we put all that behind us?" Belle pleaded. "I know I was no great shakes as a mother. But I had some damn good excuses."

She said it with a valiant attempt at a smile that she obviously didn't feel. R.J. softened in spite of himself.

"You sure as hell did," he said.

"But I've been sober for fifteen years, R.J. I really am a different person. I *detest* some of the things that other Belle Fontaine did."

And she should: She had trampled on people, stabbed fellow actors in the back, clawed her way to the top over the mangled careers of everyone who stood in her way. And her son had not always been spared.

R.J. felt her hand covering his and looked down in shock. He couldn't remember the last time she had touched him.

He looked up into those famous, gorgeous blue eyes, now wet with tears she was trying not to show.

"It may be too late to be your mother," she said, her voice not quite breaking, "but could I at least be your friend? We hardly know each other."

"It's hard to really know somebody in ninety minutes a year," he said, wanting to buy into what she was saying but not daring to, not yet, not so easily.

"You know, R.J.," she husked in her best velvet voice, "I'm trying very hard, I really am. When you get to be a certain age, family is a lot more important."

"More important than your career?" he asked her.

"Oh, God, you're a bastard when you want to be." She took her hand away. "Just like your father." She rummaged through her handbag and pulled out a tissue, dabbing at her eyes and then blowing her nose genteelly. "You even look like him when you say those things, and it makes me crazy, darling. I miss him terribly."

It was a good recovery. The use of the word "darling" was a tip-off, though. She was back in control.

That was about it. Michael came back and they waded through a miserable, awkward lunch. Sixteen people stopped and asked politely for autographs. Michael sang a few snatches of his terribly clever lyrics. A total stranger insisted on paying the check.

And R.J. staggered out an hour later, wondering at that strange interlude with his mother. She'd seemed sincere, but then Belle had made a career out of seeming sincere. And he had a nagging suspicion that he'd heard some of her lines before, in one of her old movies.

It was true that she was a different person now, sober. But he still didn't know who that person was. And, stubbornly, he felt it was up to her to let him know.

He went home uneasy about the whole thing, unwilling to believe that somebody could really change that much, and unable to dismiss the idea completely. But the uneasiness faded as he got back to work on a new case, a man who thought his wife was sleeping with his father.

It was almost a year before he thought about that lunch again, and his mother's hand reaching across the table to hold his.

And then it was too late.

CHAPTER 2

R.J. checked the illuminated dial of his Ebel watch—a gift from his partially satisfied client—and figured he'd given them long enough. With his Pentax IQ, fitted with a lens and automatic focus, he'd already gotten the girl's picture when she arrived.

Another redhead. Not as young as the old man's usual prey: college girl, no doubt, working her way through school on her back. She'd only hook until she had her B.A. Sure she would.

Tough not to be cynical on this end of the camera, R.J. thought as he snapped off half a dozen of the girl and Burkette climbing out of the car and giggling on into the townhouse.

But street shots weren't enough. The jaded magistrates of New York's matrimonial bench needed animated fuck shots. They weren't the only ones.

"I want the bastard's balls," Tina Burkette had said, handing over R.J.'s retainer.

"For the right price," he'd assured her, "I'll give 'em to you in a pickle jar for your mantel."

That had pleased her, and she wasn't shy about showing it. They'd spent a memorable evening cementing client-investigator relationships in a hot tub and a waterbed the size of Long Island Sound.

But the truth was, he didn't really give a rat's ass who or what the millionaire tycoon was shacked up with tonight in his brownstone lair near Gramercy Park. If the guy wanted to screw an albino manatee that was okay with R.J.—as long as the manatee didn't mind. But R.J. had a job to do.

He grabbed his camera, locked the car door, and crossed the street in the November gloom. It was after two A.M. and the neighborhood was deserted. It was chilly, in the upper thirties, and R.J. shivered slightly as he crossed the street.

Moving in shadows close to the building, he was almost invisible in his black jogging pants, black turtleneck sweater, and dark running shoes. A pair of wire cutters hung from his belt and infrared goggles around his neck.

He sheltered in a doorway while a man in a fur coat walked a barbered poodle across the way. The dog stopped and arched its back, then walked in a tight little circle as it forced the turds out onto the sidewalk. When it was done, the man in the fur coat stooped over and collected the turds with a plastic glove, dropping them into a Baggie.

The two walked away. R.J. slid out of the doorway, looked carefully down the street, and moved on.

In the distance, a wind-driven siren wailed near Times Square. A stolen car chase, shootout in the Garment District, more slaughter on Fifth Avenue.

But here the sidewalks were clean and safe, the buildings well-lit and professionally monitored. Only

Mafia neighborhoods were more secure. Jaguars, Caddies, and Lincoln Town Cars snuggled against the curbs. A few blocks closer to the river and they would be cannibalized before dawn.

It was a hell of a thing, what was happening to his home town, R.J. thought. Corporate raiders and subway marauders, grime and soot and social decay in every quarter. Wasn't even a good place to visit anymore.

But it got into your blood, and R.J. didn't think he could live anywhere else. Home wasn't always where you were born. He'd come east from California for college and never left. Some places you could live and never belong. But R.J. Brooks belonged in Manhattan.

He glanced at a sketch of the layout of Burkette's hideaway and hoped Tina's relationship with a member of her husband's security detail was enough to guarantee the reliability of the floor plan.

Burkette's damned bodyguard was another worry. The night before R.J. and the brute had tangled. It hadn't been much fun. R.J. would have to work fast and keep out of the big guy's way.

He shinnied up a utility pole in the alley behind the Burkette place, having already scoped out the power line that connected to the brownstone.

A phone call from the mother of his son was really eating at him. He shouldn't have popped off about the reason his support check was late this month. He'd spent his limited funds out of humanitarian concerns— the creature comforts of one R.J. Brooks. In other words, he'd eaten his customary two meals every other day whether he was hungry or not.

But this time Billie Sue wasn't talking money. It was Danny. "He's your son too," she'd said. "And you're no better daddy to him than your grand old man was to you."

R.J. cut the power line with the steel cutters from his belt. It had been a rotten thing to say, but maybe Billie Sue was right. Maybe he needed to get closer to the kid somehow. Hell, R.J. had needed somebody to show him how to behave. His son was no different—and he couldn't be getting much help from Billie Sue.

The kid was in trouble at school again, hot Cavalier blood boiling in his veins. R.J. didn't understand his son any better than he'd understood Billie Sue. What had he ever seen in that Southern flower child of his youth? Firm breasts and gentle hands. Ready mouth and white teeth nipping at the strictures of the Establishment. *Let the sun shine. Let the sun shine in.* Booze and pills. Pills and booze. Sour breath morning, noon, and night. *Let the sun shine in.*

Halfway up the pole R.J. realized he was short of breath. He tried to clear his lungs with three deep breaths. Ought to go on a diet before the Christmas glut, he thought. Maybe level off around a hundred and sixty. Mom was right: I'm carrying too much weight for 5'11". It was damned hard keeping it down, though, after getting off cigars and booze. Needed to exercise more. Live dangerously, jog in the Park.

He hadn't heard from his mother, beyond one quick phone call and a birthday card, since that lunch almost a year before. He hadn't spent much time feeling bad about that, either.

R.J. heard a renewed burst of sirens from uptown and looked at his watch. Twenty minutes had passed. They must be getting it on by now. He made his way off the pole and onto the lip of a stone fence that enclosed the brownstone's garden.

He sneezed, almost falling. Then he sneezed again—four, five, six times before the eruption subsided. A goddamn serial sneezer. He struggled to keep his balance until his eyes cleared. Christ, he'd be shot for sport by the first insomniac who poked his head outside for a breath of fresh air pollution.

To have come to this, he thought, shaking his head at the stereotyped movie image of the jaundiced private eye. Burning cigarettes dangling from the corner of his mouth, dark glass of rotgut cradled in his hands, the tinny clink of piano keys in the hazy lounge of some gin joint on the other side of the world. Waiting for *her* to walk in, see . . .

He moved along the lip of the fence toward the drainpipe that ran from ground level up the side of the building. Who was he trying to kid? He hated what he did, but he was exactly where he wanted to be. It suited him. He wanted this outsider independence. He trusted no man, woman, or institution to shape his existence. The world was a mess, and most people were going to hell in a handbasket. That was all right with him. He'd even helped a few get there.

"I'm a simple guy," he'd told Tina Burkette when she hired him. "I have a job to do. I go at it the most direct way I know. One step at a time. Eventually I get where I'm going." They'd been heading for the hot tub in the Burkette mansion on Long Island. "You know what he'd do to you," Tina had giggled while she decorated him with bubbles, "if he catch you paddling in my bath water?"

R.J. shifted an unlit cigar to the other side of his mouth and stepped off the fence onto a wall bracket that secured the drainpipe. He almost lost his footing as a face peered at him from a window—his reflection. Sam Spade, my ass. He looked more like a cat burglar with delusions of grandeur. He had his fictional mentor's devil streak, all right, and the jutting jaw line, but his eyes were cobalt blue, like his mother's; and although he could talk as tough as his crusty old man when the chips were down, he usually tried to reason his way out of scrapes before resorting to rough stuff.

But there were some burdens you just couldn't run away from. Genetics, for one thing. Some said he had his mother's sultry mannerisms, and what he remembered of his combative father's knotted physique and eccentric lisp. But he'd also shared their devotion to strong drink.

He wondered briefly why he was thinking about his parents and tried to bring his mind back to the job before he fell off and got a fence post up his ass. I could use a shot now, he thought, licking at the dryness in his mouth. Rye, Scotch, bourbon. Crankcase oil.

He clutched the drainpipe and pulled his other foot away from the fence, hoping the pipe would support his weight. Hanging there, he rubbed nervous perspiration out of the scar-dimple on his chin, the result of a childhood car accident, and felt his pulse quicken as he considered the part booze had played in his life. Relationships destined to self-destruct were at the top of the list.

A self-recovered alcoholic, R.J. hadn't gotten high on anything but a little weed in a decade. But where was being sober getting him? In those years he'd seen it all: adulterous spouses, bestial employers, crooked unionists, representatives of the cloth with a taste for altar boys, and corrupt government officials at every level. He exercised his talents in a human cesspool.

Maybe he should pack it all in and take the kid down to Key West. Buy into one of those charter boat outfits. Live a life of sun, sea, and middle-class normality. Forget the Tina Burkettes and their precious spoils. Forget Billie Sue's anger. Forget his unforgettable mother and father. Forget—

He almost jumped over the fence when a garage door across the alley slammed and a car engine suddenly fired up.

It was time to get moving. The old man would be approaching paydirt by now. The bodyguard was probably on his second shot with the Puerto Rican housekeeper downstairs in the servants' quarters.

R.J. slipped his infrared goggles into place and eased onto the wrought-iron railing of the balcony.

Uptown at a posh Manhattan hotel, an aging house detective swallowed thickly. "Jaysus," he said. "Imagine getting it like that. Right in the saddle."

The murdered couple lay entangled on a massage table in the bathroom, almost as if their positions had been staged. The woman's silky blond hair fanned out over one shoulder, where fresh blood stained a rose-shaped birthmark.

"Don't touch anything," warned the first policeman to arrive. "Crime Scene Unit will rip me a new one if I mess this one up."

"Don't I know it?" said the house dick. "Wasn't I twenty-three years on the Force myself?"

"And then you got caught, huh?" said the cop. The house detective turned away. That was a little too close to the truth for his liking.

"Looks like the same bullet got 'em both," the cop went on, bending over to get a better look without moving closer.

"No shit," said the house man, still sulking a little, "but the shooter popped her another one for good measure. Look at the goo above her ear—two bits says there's a hunk of lead in there."

The woman had been forced forward over the man's splayed body by the back wound. Her chin rested on his forehead with her face turned away from the door. Her eyes were open.

A rose had been jammed into the bullet wound, and

a handful of Polaroid pictures were fanned out around her.

"Huh," the house man said. "Anyway, looks like somebody had a good time with her first." He nodded at the marks along much of the visible skin on the woman's back. "Did that with pliers, most likely." He shook his head. "I remember, must have been eighteen, nineteen years ago—"

"Holy shit," the young cop interrupted. "I just got a good look at her face. Over there in the mirror, look-it—see what I mean?"

"Sure, they must have been watching everything they was doing while they was doin' it. I wonder if they saw the killer." He glanced at the young cop and noticed the kid's eyes were still bugging out. "Say, what the hell's the matter with you, kid? This your first stiff or something?"

The young cop turned popping eyes on the older man. "Jesus Christ, man—don't you know who she used to be?"

———————◆———————

The balcony outside the window was no larger than the cheapest box seat on Broadway. R.J. shivered at the thought, remembering the last show he'd gone to with his mother. He hated the theater, and her artsy-fartsy friends, her whole world. There hadn't been any use trying to pretend. He'd had an awful time and she knew it.

It was pitch black on the balcony, but with his goggles in place he saw a reddish glow through the window. Heat radiated from the naked bodies inside. No sign of the dreaded bodyguard. Last night the hulk had slipped up on R.J. when he'd been parked at the end of the block, watching the brownstone. Wearing jackboots, a bomber jacket, and the glazed look of a steroidal linebacker, he'd tapped on R.J.'s window.

"Man's getting pissed, see?" the goon had said, sounding like an adenoidal pit bull. "He don't like all this cat-and-mouse shit. Says why don't you just ask for what you want like a man." He flipped a Polaroid into R.J.'s lap. "This the kind of stuff you're looking for?"

R.J. frowned at the image of a man and woman in criminal conversation in a sudsy hot tub. He looked pretty good, but the picture just didn't do justice to Mrs. Burkette. Anyway, the message was clear: Fuck Off.

"If I leave now, will your boss punch my time clock?" he asked. The bodyguard didn't laugh. Instead, without taking his eyes off R.J.'s, he reached down and grabbed the frame of the car.

He shook. So did the car. His eyes were narrow and close-set like a nun's.

R.J. took a deep breath as his car did a samba against the curb. His weapon of choice was a Bulldog .44 Special, short, ugly, hammer-bobbed and barrel vented near the muzzle to cut down on the jarring recoil. He wore it clipped behind his belt. Some of his colleagues thought it was a bit much, but R.J. liked the security of having his special edge—the Big E, he called it. He never drew the weapon unless he meant to use it. But he never gave a crook an even break.

He was thinking hard about jamming the Big E down this over-muscled bozo's throat when the man snarled, "Get outta that car!" He reached for R.J.'s door handle.

R.J. put a hand under the dashboard and flipped a switch. His theft alarm started screaming, a sound like a Nazi klaxon from an old black-and-white thriller.

The bodyguard froze, then frantically looked around. "Crazy sonofabitch," he mumbled, backing into the shadows nervously, "I'll get you for this."

R.J. wasn't looking forward to another confrontation. With a wary glance inside, he tested the window's latch. It wasn't locked. He wouldn't have to break the glass. As he eased it open, he could hear them sloshing around on the water bed.

"Oh, God," Burkette groaned. "Oh my fucking God. I came so hard I've gone blind."

"I think something happened to the lights," said the boy in the long red wig.

Through R.J.'s goggles the scene was surreal. Heat waves pulsated from their limbs like special effects in a Spielberg movie. The boy was propped on one elbow with the tycoon's receding penis in his hand. He stared in amazement at the apparition by the window.

Suddenly R.J.'s flashbulbs popped in their faces, blinding them again.

"What the hell!" The tycoon bolted upright and shoved the boy onto the floor.

R.J. could see the man's fear. He moved quickly to the foot of the bed, snapping off another frame.

"Jesus!" Burkette screamed, digging at his eyes.

Passing quickly to the other side of the bed, R.J. took another flash shot, catching the boy's girlish buttocks in profile as he bent to find his undershorts on the floor.

R.J. heard a ruckus outside the door.

"Mr. Burkette?" he could hear the bodyguard lumbering and panting up the stairs in the darkness.

"Get your ass in here!" yelled the tycoon, rolling off his side of the bed.

As the bodyguard splintered through the door like an enraged rhino, R.J. stepped right over to him and shot a flash in the startled man's face. He followed up with a jab to the sternum and a hard shove. The bodyguard fell back into the hall.

"Do something!" Burkette demanded of his bed companion, backing away as fast and as far across the room as he could.

Through his goggles, R.J. saw the boy's smile in the darkness. He was unafraid, having realized that R.J. meant him no harm. His wig was askew, his willowy body rigid with the theatrical excitement of it all. His eyes widened and he wet his lips with sensual appreciation of the moment.

R.J. shook his head and stepped to the window. "The lawyers will work things out," he said, and was over the railing before they realized he was gone.

The bodyguard's voice caught up with him in the alley. "I'll have your ass for this!"

R.J. looked back through his goggles. The bodyguard was still naked except for his unlaced jackboots.

R.J. snapped off another flash. "Gotcha," he said.

CHAPTER 3

He was asleep with a naked blonde in his arms when the intruder picked his lock and came in like a cat burglar at dawn's first light.

R.J.'s apartment sat in an old four-story building in the East Seventies. You could hear cockroaches walking across the loose floorboards. R.J. eased out of bed in his pajamas. What he heard was a hell of a lot bigger than a cockroach. He slipped behind the bedroom door and waited.

When the intruder glided in, R.J. chopped him on the neck. The man wilted, semi-paralyzed by the blow. R.J. held onto his collar and turned on the light.

"Hijo de puta!"

"What the hell are you doing here?" R.J. asked.

"Came to see you," Henry Portillo groaned. He rubbed his neck, struggling to bring things back in focus. *"Hijo de puta mas grande en el mundo* . . . Did I teach you to hit like that?" He stood upright and slipped a plastic credit card back into his wallet.

"Yeah, you did."

He shook his head. "I am a better teacher than I thought. That hurt, *chico*. It still hurts."

The girl on the bed frowned and muttered something that might have been mean. She turned toward the wall and pulled the pillow over her tousled head. Her buttocks were dimpled, and a nautical tattoo fluttered between her cheeks.

R.J. saw him glance at Gloria and could see his jaw muscles tighten in disapproval.

R.J. reached for the habitual cigar he'd not put a match to in several years. "Gloria," he said. "An old friend."

Henry shook his head. "We need to talk. Alone."

Portillo's *mestizo* face was as brown as desert sand. Despite fifty years in the United States, he still spoke with a slight accent of his native Guadalajara. A stocky, clean-shaven man, he wore corduroy jeans, a Viyella shirt and suede jacket, and hand-tooled Mexican leather boots. His belt buckle and bolero tie clasp were mosaics of beaten Aztec gold and silver. He'd dropped his Stetson on the couch, and R.J. noticed his luxurious mane had turned more salt than pepper since he'd seen him last.

R.J. pulled the covers over Gloria's backside. "We can talk out there," he said, motioning to the living room.

He wasn't about to explain his conduct, even to his Uncle Hank. Gloria was a friend from the local police precinct, a radio operator in the dispatch office. He'd done her a favor during her first divorce, and tonight she'd discovered her new husband and rogue about town in bed with another woman. Distraught, she'd been waiting on the doorstep when R.J. got home from the Burkette surveillance.

He'd given her a drink and a shoulder to cry on, and they'd talked the rest of the night. Even when her despair had turned to anger and the need for revenge, he'd refused to take advantage of her. She'd come on to him, doing a slow, seductive strip—showing him the most enticing tush he'd seen in a long time. But he'd managed to keep her off balance until she'd passed out.

Let Hank think what he wanted. He always had.

"What are you doing in New York, anyway?" R.J. said, pouring a glass of orange juice into a Mets souvenir beer stein. "Los Angeles run out of crime?" He knocked back the juice like a shot of rye, then eased off the cold linoleum floor to warm his bare feet on the living-room carpet.

"I've been working with the FBI Behavioral Science Unit at Quantico," Portillo said. "Caught the shuttle to New York this morning to see you."

"Nice. What is it, two years?"

"Eighteen months," the older man grated. R.J. was a little surprised at the flinty tone of voice.

"Okay, eighteen months. A long time, anyway."

Portillo glanced through the open bedroom door at Gloria. "Things don't seem to have changed very much."

R.J. was annoyed at the judgment in his uncle's voice. "Get it off your hairy chest, Uncle Hank. Why are you really here?"

The older detective's baked expression hardened. "Your mother's dead," he said.

For a long moment R.J. didn't move or speak. He could feel the blood drain from his face and puddle in his feet. He swallowed hard. "People die, Hank. Even in sunny California, people die."

Tears gleamed in the corners of Henry Portillo's eyes. "Your mother died last night here. In New York City. She was murdered."

R.J.'s head jerked back as if he'd been struck. Portillo drew a folded newspaper from his coat and spread it on the coffee table.

The headline read:

**FILM LEGEND BELLE FONTAINE MURDERED
IN LOVE NEST**
Unknown Killer Still at Large

CHAPTER 4

"You shouldn't be alone at a time like this, kid." Uncle Hank picked up his Stetson and paused at the door. "If you won't talk with me, go see somebody you can talk to."

"I've been alone all my life," R.J. said. "Why should this be different?"

Portillo blanched. "Thank you for that," he said and closed the door.

R.J. wanted to go after him but couldn't move. Portillo had left the early edition of the *Times* open on the coffee table, the headline facing up. There was nothing else R.J. needed to know.

His mother was dead.

He stared at the peeling paint on the closed door and thought about adding a new deadbolt to keep unwanted visitors out.

Jesus. What a rotten thing to say—to Hank Portillo, of all people. The man had been a rock for R.J., a surrogate father. Never pushy, but always there. And he'd left his work in Quantico to bring the news, so R.J. wouldn't have to hear it from a stranger.

His thoughts swirled like leaves in an autumn wind. No: Not just because of me.

Uncle Hank hadn't come all this way only for his benefit. R.J. knew—had always known. Hank loved her, even before the death of R.J.'s father. It was the kind of thing a child knew and an adult was so dumb about. Hank loved her. He remembered unspoken words, gestures, glances. He wondered if his father had ever seen it. He wondered if Belle had known.

Belle Fontaine. Star of stage and screen. Wife and mother. I loved her too, R.J. thought with inexplicable fierceness. *I loved her too*.

And now she was dead. Murdered. He looked at the photograph on the front page: the blond, lustrous hair, the searing blue eyes, the strong willowy body. He gagged and raced for the bathroom.

He rinsed his mouth and washed his face with a cold cloth. He stood at the mirror, unmoving, scarcely breathing. Looking into his mother's eyes.

"Honey? You got another chick stashed away in here?"

He moved his eyes to Gloria's reflection in the mirror as she snatched back the shower curtain and pretended to look for another woman. Gloria wore pearl earbobs and R.J.'s tattered bedroom slippers and damn little else. She struck a pose and pouted at him. "Somebody you like a whole lot better'n you like me, from the way I got treated last night."

He shook his head, watching as she stepped into the stall and turned on the water.

"I knew you wouldn't take advantage of me, though—me drunk and with the blues so bad." She stretched out her arms through the cascading water.

"But I'm not drunk now, and I don't feel bad at all."

He moved into her instinctive embrace, burying his face in the crook of her neck, letting the water run over him. "Oh, baby, baby," she crooned. "What's the matter? Tell mama what's the matter."

But R.J. just stood for a long moment, letting the water soak his clothes.

The lounge over on 42nd Street was a mistake.

There was a TV set behind the bar. It was blasting out the news, polluted with facts and lies about Belle Fontaine. A local producer named Casey Wingate had been doing a profile on his mother at the time of her death, and an abbreviated version of it was getting a lot of play. R.J. had left before he finished his drink.

Now, sitting in a back booth on the dark side of Jago's Restaurant and Bar near the old Chrysler Building, he nursed a bottle of rye under the disapproving, one-eyed scowl of Peter McInerny. In the last decade, the "Pirate" had served R.J. through the delirium of drink and the horrors of sobriety.

He couldn't remember the last time he'd had a drink. But then, he couldn't remember the last time his mother had been killed either.

In the flesh, that is. He'd seen her die many times in celluloid, larger-than-life fade-outs. He remembered the first time. Maizie, their maid, had taken him to a theater near the ranch house in Brentwood. An aspiring actress, she believed that Belle Fontaine would open the right doors for her.

The movie was *Blood on the Sun*. His mother had looked so pretty. He was only five or six, but he could still recall the way she walked, the smoky sound of her voice, and the way her eyes misted over whenever a scene required emotion. He remembered her dimpled smile, sun-lit hair blowing in the breeze on the deck of a small cabin cruiser. The action was supposed to take place on the China coast, but he had recognized numerous California landmarks, even at that tender age.

In the movie his mother came up from the cabin in a tailored fatigue uniform, something to do with the war effort. She was met simultaneously by the love of her life and a hail of Japanese machine-gun bullets. Close-up. Fade-out. The End.

It had taken three hours and a double sedative for his mother to get him to sleep that night. Maizie was sent packing the next morning, and R.J. was sure she hadn't bothered to ask for a reference.

That was the first time. There had been a lot of others. Over the years he'd gotten used to seeing his mother die, and that was part of the shock he was feeling now.

Because this time the death was real. So said Uncle Hank, the police, and the medical examiner. And a TV producer named Casey Wingate. He frowned. There was something disturbing about that piece of film he'd seen in the other bar. . . .

A face. A familiar form. Some shadow from the past—

No. It was no good. He couldn't grab hold of it, bring it into focus.

Maybe it was just that he'd been drinking for the last few hours. Maybe that had driven it all out of his head.

But R.J. had a bad feeling that even if he stopped drinking he would not remember. It was too shadowy, too elusive—

"Why don't you go on home, R.J.? You had enough to drink."

The waitress was the only person he'd known since Billie Sue who could stretch a one-syllable word into three. She was a teenager who hadn't shed the Georgia shantytown of her birth. "Doreen, there's no such thing as enough to drink," he said.

Experience told him he was in shock, that he had to fight it or go back under. He made an awkward effort to straighten his collar and brushed away the blade of hair slashing across his forehead. His clothes were a mess, his eyes scorched.

"You want some comp'ny, then? It ain't good to drink alone."

"Gotta do it alone, sweetheart. Like living. Like dying." He took a belt of whiskey and shuddered like a wet dog.

Doreen wiped his table. "You jes' let me know if I can help," she said and went behind the bar to talk with McInerny.

R.J. saw their reflections in the beveled mirror. The Pirate would foul his whiskey with water for the rest of the voyage. Damn.

Doreen's heart was in the right place, though. She was a good kid. They all were. He'd never met a cocktail waitress he didn't like. R.J.'s mother had been a cocktail waitress in the old days, between high school and movie stardom. He remembered a picture of her in a movie magazine, wearing a skimpy cocktail outfit with a cotton tail on her cute behind.

R.J. remembered a lot of things about his mother. In particular he remembered that last strange lunch with her almost a year ago. Her reaching out to him. Him not believing it.

He sniffed the lingering fumes in his glass. At least he wouldn't have to identify the body. Uncle Hank had seen to that. Just like he'd been seeing to so many things for thirty-some years, since that day he'd noticed the lonely boy on the movie set and taken him under his wiry brown wing.

And he'd been there ever since. When R.J. got into

trouble at school, it was Henry Portillo who showed up to whip him into line. Belle was too busy, of course, although Uncle Hank would not listen to R.J.'s bitterness about that.

And when R.J. finally graduated, it was Henry Portillo who sat on the cheap folding chair with a Kodak and a proud smile.

He was always there, always doing the dirty work when Belle was too busy—always—and when R.J. needed a friend.

R.J. was glad to have him do the dirty work now. The police would have come knocking at R.J.'s door had they known of the blood relationship, but R.J. used neither parent's name in his profession. He'd have to face them sooner or later, but he would just as soon steer clear of the police for a day or two.

The door opened and a gust of wind-driven rain blew into the room, ripping the smoke apart. Disgruntled voices moaned and cursed, and a man in the next booth yelled an obscenity, then boxed his companion on the arm. She was thin, with stringy bleached hair and dark circles under her eyes that even her heavy makeup couldn't hide. He was just an everyday jerk.

"What the hell was that for?" the girl complained, rubbing her arm. R.J. heard their conversation beneath the plaintive voice of Michael Bolton from the jukebox.

"Give us a kiss," the jerk growled.

"Okay, but cut the rough stuff. I don't like it that way."

"Sure, baby. Call me Rex."

"You wanna play rough, Rex, I got a girlfriend who specializes. I can give you her number."

"Don't get all riled up. Here, see how this feels. A hogsleg a girl can get a handle on."

"Wow," she said, her hand sliding under the table, "that's a big one all right."

Jesus, thought R.J. It was time to leave. He pushed himself up from the table—and bumped into hard steel.

"Where you going, gumshoe?"

In the dark room R.J. could see little more than the whites of the man's eyes. He jumped back reflexively.

"Don't *do* that, Hookshot! Sneak up on me like that, you'll get a goddam bullet between the eyes one a these days."

White teeth flashed to match the eyes. "Buy me a beer."

"Buy your own goddamn beer. You got more money than I'll see in a hundred years."

Wallace "Hookshot" Steigler signaled the Pirate for a beer, then leaned his gaunt frame into the booth across from R.J. He was dressed in black and looked like a bird of prey—a bird with one steel wing. He put the hook that had replaced his right hand on the table with a thunk.

"Sorry about your mother," he said.

R.J. nodded, and Doreen brought their drinks, pausing to touch the gleaming steel hook like she couldn't quite help herself. She caught herself and looked at Hookshot guiltily.

"Help yourself, darlin'," Hookshot told her. "No thrill like the feel of steel." He smiled as Doreen shivered and backed away.

"One of these days," Hookshot said when she was gone. The way he said it implied things way beyond kinky that R.J. couldn't even imagine. He laughed in spite of his mood.

"You're dreaming," he told Hookshot and laughed again. He could always count on Hookshot for a laugh.

That was one of the reasons he loved him.

Wallace Steigler was a Jewish black man. His father had been assigned to the United Nations when Israel was called Palestine and wasn't a nation yet. He'd been one of a small band of men lobbying for votes for the Jewish state. A tough man, hardened by half a life of fighting.

At a cocktail party on the East side he'd met Hookshot's mother, a Harlem beauty who took away his breath and his common sense with their first kiss. He was killed by an Arab League assassin a month after their son was born.

Growing up in Harlem, young Wallace had displayed a tremendous talent for basketball, until a run-in on the wrong turf had left him without his shooting hand.

Lean to the point of cadaverousness, Hookshot was without apparent age. He might have been forty, fifty, even sixty. Nobody knew for sure. He had managed a news kiosk in Midtown Manhattan for thirty years. He knew every man, woman, and child who'd ever dealt with him, and quite a few who hadn't. His kiosk was an unofficial base for intelligence drops on both sides of the law. Besides Uncle Hank, Hookshot was the only real friend R.J. had.

"I don't like to intrude at a time like this—"

"But you will."

Hookshot looked away. "Hank's worried. Says you didn't take the news too good."

"I'll try to do better next time."

Hookshot ignored the sarcasm. "Gloria said she didn't know where you went."

R.J. shrugged. "A rainy day in Central Park." Even to his own ears his voice was filled with whiskey-phlegm and the gut-wracking ache of self-reproach. He belted his watered-down drink and signaled for Doreen.

As R.J. reached for the fresh drink, the steel hook trapped his wrist. "You don't need anymore, man, you had too much when you uncorked the bottle."

"I need your advice I'll ask for it," R.J. said. "You got a cigar?"

"Don't need any smokes, either. You've done enough wallowing to get ready for what you got to do."

"Got nothing special to do. Burkette case is about finished. I might take a vacation. Miami, Bermuda, Trinidad. Sun and sand and sea."

Hookshot frowned. "Hank says they don't have a make on the dead man with her yet. Killer might not have been after Belle at all. Maybe the man's wife went nuts or something. Or maybe he was running an overdue tab with a bookie. Those boys get grouchy when you come up short. Anyhow, I'm putting out feelers."

"Steel feelers?"

"Okay, you the pro. What do you think happened?"

R.J. shook his head. "Go away, Hookshot. Not tonight."

Hookshot leaned in toward R.J. "Especially tonight."

R.J. pulled back and waved his glass at Doreen, but Hookshot waved her off. "Come on, man, what are you gonna do about this?"

"Go to another bar if they won't serve me here anymore."

"The murder, man."

"Let the police do something. That's what we pay 'em for."

Hookshot's lips curled into a snarl. "You trust them with something this important to you?"

R.J. glared at his friend, who leaned his gaunt face

across the table, growling like a small animal.

"There's a killer out there," Hookshot said deliberately. "A murderer on the loose. Feeling like he got away with one. And it's your mama. He killed your mama. She's dead, you're alive. Time to stop feeling sorry for yourself. Get off your skinny white ass and *do* something."

R.J. straightened his shoulders. The murky film over his eyes faded. Hookshot noticed the response and leaned back slightly.

"All right. That's better. Now let's get outta here. We'll go to my place and talk. Hook up with Hank, see what he knows. He's been to see the cops. And he tried to find that TV producer, Casey Wingate, the one been digging up stuff on your mother."

But R.J. shook his head. "Not tonight."

Hookshot glared at him, then stood up. "Suit yourself," he said coldly. He took a step toward the door.

"Hey, Rufus, how you pick your nose with that thing?" It was Rex, the redhot lover in the next booth. Hookshot moved to go around him, but Rex stuck out a leg to stop him. "I hear you coloreds are so talented down there. How you shake yours out when you pee? Got holes in it from that banana hook?"

The waitress, Doreen, came over and stood between them. Rex snaked an arm around her and grabbed Hookshot by the jacket front. "I asked you a question, Spook."

Hookshot looked at him. "Let go my jacket." It was a black silk jacket. Hookshot loved it and was never without it.

"Let him go," Doreen said. Rex looked at her, smiled, and let go of the jacket.

"Maybe this boy wants to make me," he said.

Hookshot shook his head and stepped around them.

R.J. pushed aside his glass and stood up. He glared

at Rex, who was grinning, looking proudly at his "date." Doreen stayed between R.J. and Rex until R.J. moved away to the bar to pay his tab. Hookshot stood waiting by the exit.

R.J. walked over to his friend.

"You go ahead, Hookshot. I'll catch up with you later."

"R.J., man, let it go. I already have. Look, the jacket's not even wrinkled. Come on with me now."

"Go on," he insisted.

Hookshot gave him a long look, then sighed and left, shaking his head. R.J. stood at the bar, waiting. Pirate served him a double soda on the rocks, and Doreen caressed his shoulder each time she passed.

When Sexy Rex finally went to the can, R.J. was right behind him. When R.J. flushed the toilet, Rex's head was in the bowl and the voice of Lee Greenwood was affirming how great it was to be an American.

CHAPTER 5

*T*he reflection in the big mirror behind the bar is perfect. A dark-haired, ruddy-faced, middle-aged man in British tweeds is sitting rigidly at the bar, sipping his second brandy and soda in front of the beveled mirror. The same stool. Same one-eyed bartender. Same waitress.

And they don't know him.

His blood churns like river rapids. Belle's son had been so deflated. It is always thrilling to see their faces afterwards. Hear their voices. The survivors. The ones left behind.

It is a mystical process, the way he makes his way into their orbits, before and after. He comes and goes in their lives and they never know he is there. Until it is too late.

But this had been the best, the absolute best. A payoff he had never dared hope for, falling right into his lap. Something so perfect—it was clearly more than coincidence. Had to be. It was meant to be, from the beginning. The long wait had only made the payoff more perfect.

The son had roused himself, sufficient to deal with the fool in the bathroom. But it wouldn't last. He would lash out in pain and confusion, then subside into that wonderful dead apathy, crushed by the weight of his loss.

He finishes his drink and nudges the glass across the bar.

He feels godlike. He likes the feeling.

He has always liked the feeling.

On Third Avenue R.J. paused to clear his head and hail a taxi. His blood was still toxic but he was coming around. A little brisk exercise after drinking always cleared his head better than coffee.

Hookshot was right. Enough to drink; things to do now, and he needed a clear head to do them. His desire for any more to drink had shrunk, dwindled away to a small kitten next to the raging lion that had been inside him earlier.

He could handle it now. He was that kind of boozer: drink when he wanted and stop when he was ready. It was hard, but he was no goddamn alky, no matter what anybody said.

He took a deep breath of city air and coughed it right back up. It was cold, and he smelled rain around the corner. He didn't mind rain or cold, especially when he was working. And R.J. Brooks was working.

He'd known he had to do something, even when he was saying he wouldn't. After all, it was his mother. It didn't matter whether she was a great mother or what he thought of her. She was his mother, for Christ's sake. And if your mother was murdered, you had to do something about it.

A taxi pulled up to the curb beside him. He waved it off. He could think better on his feet. He was sure he could make it home before the rain.

R.J. turned up his collar and began to walk. He got into a good steady rhythm, hands in his pockets, shoulders hunched against the wind.

He was in the mid-Sixties when he forgot all about the weather.

The dark Mercedes screeched in off the street and nearly pinned him against the side of a restaurant. "Jesus!" he shouted, cracking his elbow against the stone wall as he jumped for safety.

The two men in black leather who jumped out of the car were on him so fast he could only try to cover up, not fight back. He felt the first couple of blows, then nothing much at all until an old wino poked at his face with a greasy handkerchief. "What the hell . . . ?"

"Easy, fella." The old man looked like a worn rake handle. Rags hung off his bones like tattered wrapping paper, and his fingers worked with the crackle of oilskin. "Better take it easy, you don't wanna spend the rest of the night up to Bellevue."

His head was pounding, and he could see his blood on the crusty rag when the wino took it away from his face.

"Those guys—who were they?"

"What guys?"

"The guys who just kicked the shit out of me."

The wino shook his head, or maybe it always shook like that. "You got it bad, kid?"

R.J. stumbled to the sidewalk. The mist thickened. His jacket was ripped, a hole in the knee of his pants. His whole body throbbed dully. "What time is it?" The air frosted in front of his face as he spoke.

"Don't know anything about time," the wino said. "It's dark."

"And here comes the rain," said R.J.

"You wanna come with me, I got a place down by the river."

R.J. took a step and staggered against a lightpost, bracing his arm for support. "I'm okay. I got a place. Thanks."

He took a deep breath, then tried a few steps. His knee was stiff and a couple of ribs were bruised. He could feel clotted blood on his cheekbone. His ears throbbed from a dozen punches.

At first he'd thought it might be Rex and one of his asshole buddies. But it was Burkette's bodyguard, with a pal riding shotgun.

R.J. had walked right into it, eyes blurred by whiskey and self-pity. He was lucky it wasn't a whole lot worse.

He dug a pair of tens out of his pocket. "You're good people, pops. I won't forget it."

The old man looked at the money and nearly fainted.

CHAPTER 6

For three days he stayed in the apartment with his tabby cat, Ilsa. He didn't go out, didn't see or talk to anyone. He read the newspapers and watched TV. He taped everything about his mother's death on his VCR. Over and over, he watched the news reports and Casey Wingate's biographical portrait.

Something still bothered him. A man in the crowd of gawkers outside the hotel when his mother's body was taken away. Very nondescript sort of guy, no reason to notice him—except R.J. *did* notice him, and couldn't figure out why, except that he must have seen him somewhere before.

So what? What did it mean?

He didn't know. But he intended to find out, as soon as he healed up a bit, at least to the point where he didn't walk like an old man.

It took two days. The first morning when he woke up it took him half an hour to get out of bed. All his muscles hurt and his head felt like a bowling ball on a swivel. He took a lot of naps and sipped on some bouillon.

The second day was worse. All the aches, pains, and bruises had gotten stiff. Trying to make his body do something was like operating strange machinery with worn controls. He spent much of the day in bed again, or in the easy chair with the television on. He took three long, hot baths, hoping the heat would loosen up the aches. More bouillon, two slices of toast.

For breakfast on the third day he had hot tea and honey with dry toast. Lunch was a cup of yogurt. For dinner he managed a small broiled steak, tossed salad, and baked potato. He drank bottled water. Ilsa stayed out of his way.

That night a friend on the nursing staff at Lenox Hill Hospital came in to look at his wounds, patch him up, and give him a rain check for carnal intimacies when he was back on his feet.

He didn't go to the office or even phone in. But Wanda called and left random messages on the answering machine. They got a little meaner each time.

"And if I didn't feel so sorry for you because you're obviously stupid from a blow on the head, I'd walk out of this office for good, and let you find some other idiot to take your abuse. As if you could. As if anybody else *would*.

"Lieutenant Kates has called seven times. Second place to Mrs. Burkette, with three calls. She wants to know if you're all right, and do you need another meeting to discuss details." Wanda cleared her throat, or maybe it was a laugh.

"Henry Portillo called, but he didn't leave a message. Only one collection agency called, so business is good. You should drop by and see for yourself." And she hung up abruptly.

On the fourth day, R.J. ate scrambled eggs and bacon and started exercising. Situps, pushups, crunches, leg lifts—the whole regimen. It hurt like hell but he forced himself to keep moving the muscles, working through the soreness until he finally felt a little bit of his old supple strength coming back.

Afterwards he jogged a mile downtown and walked back. He took a cold shower, standing under the icy water as long as he could stand it. He toweled off. Before he got dressed he examined his body and face in the mirror.

Bruised ear, short hairline cut in the eyebrow. A jagged abrasion on his right cheekbone counterpointed the scar-dimple in his chin. A couple of dull purple spots along the rib cage, knee still slightly swollen. Nothing permanent, nothing so awful he couldn't live with it.

He shaved and brushed his teeth, ran his fingers through his damp hair. Time for a haircut, but that would keep, too.

He dressed in stone-washed jeans and a crew-necked sweater, then filled Ilsa's bowl with Friskies. He clipped the Big E onto his belt at the base of his spine, threw on a jacket and went out.

At the corner of Columbus and 72nd Street he called the office.

"Where've you been, boss?" Wanda demanded. "Everybody's looking for you."

"Just so they don't all find me at the same time," he said. A fierce looking Rastafarian appeared outside the booth and glared at him through the glass.

"Hookshot said he saw you the other night. We were worried."

"Not to worry, kid. Any hot messages?"

He watched the Rasta's antics as Wanda worked the list. He wasn't really paying attention; the Rasta was more interesting. But then he heard Wanda read off a name that caught his interest.

"Jackson Yates?" R.J. had never done any business with the society lawyer and didn't know him. He was too high-class for R.J.'s kind of work, and they didn't exactly socialize in the same places. "What's he want with me?"

"Ask him, if you ever get around to doing any business ever again. And Lieutenant Kates wants you to call him, like now."

The Rasta tapped on the glass with a ring the size of a golf ball, pointing at the telephone. He wore a pearl earring in one nostril, and three strands of bright beads around his neck. His hair was braided into dreadlocks, and freckles spotted his orange complexion, making him look like a speckled perch out of water.

"Okay, here's what you do," R.J. said, ignoring the pest. "Call Ms. Burkette and tell her the job's finished, that she'll be okay. I'll send my final artwork and a bill to her lawyer in a couple of days."

The Rasta walked off a few steps, muttering to himself, then charged back and kicked the door.

"And call Kates. I want to see him too, later this morning. Tell him it's about the Fontaine case."

"Belle Fontaine? Are you mixed up in that?"

"Just tell him."

The Rasta got a running start and rammed a shoulder into the folding door so hard it jammed R.J. against the phone box. Sharp pain flashed through his bruised ribs.

"Boss, you been seeing something of that Fontaine woman I don't know about?"

R.J. looked at the wild-eyed specimen in the now-open doorway of the booth. He was breathing hard, filled with righteous indignation. He raised a finger to speak, and R.J. cracked him on the forehead with the handpiece of the phone. The Rasta folded to the ground like a bag of psychedelic laundry.

"See you later, kid," he said and hung up.

He stepped over the soiled heap on the sidewalk and headed downtown.

At 66th Street he hailed a cab. The incident at the phone booth had got his adrenaline pumping. When he climbed out at Gramercy Park he left the door open and leaned back in to the driver.

"Wait for me."

"Your money, Mac."

R.J. was not fond of taxi drivers. He also disliked politicians, theatrical bigshots, corporate giants, racists, and militant feminists. But even more than that, he disliked having somebody think they were one up on him. It was bad for business.

"Special delivery," he told the uniformed doorman at the elegant brownstone. He stood aside as a young woman pushed a baby carriage to the sidewalk.

"I'll have to see," the doorman said, giving him a suspicious once-over.

"Go ahead and see," R.J. said, handing him a business card and smiling at the woman.

The doorman got on the intercom, unconsciously pulling at the seat of his twill pants. About twenty seconds later the door opened and Burkette's pock-faced bodyguard came out with a swagger and a smirk.

"You lookin' pretty rough there, gumshoe. Wanna exchange some photographs, or what?" he said, leaning against the door frame, arms folded.

"Or what," said R.J., grabbing him by the testicles

and squeezing. He pulled. Wide-eyed, the bodyguard followed.

The woman stopped the baby carriage and watched the grim-faced bodyguard follow R.J. down the steps with a strange, crablike motion.

On the sidewalk they squatted eyeball to eyeball beside a fire hydrant. R.J. just grinned and continued to squeeze, twisting the man's gonads in a viselike grip.

He never said a word, just shifted the cold cigar to the other side of his mouth and kept holding the man's attention.

Finally he stood and pulled the bodyguard over to a stone staircase leading to the servants' entrance and heaved him headfirst down the steps. The bodyguard landed in a cluster of garbage cans with his hands clutched between his legs. He lay there without moving.

R.J. walked back to the cab, pausing to wink at the doorman. "He might want to borrow some of the kid's diapers," he said.

The mother laughed nervously and moved away quickly.

"Man," said the cab driver as R.J. slid back in, "you got to be the craziest motherfucker in New York City."

R.J. slammed the door and settled back on the seat.

"Don't know about that," he said, spitting the cigar stub out the window, "but I feel like the meanest."

CHAPTER 7

R.J. spent an hour in the office. Rain pelted the window behind his metal desk, blurring his view of the building across the street. The window had venetian blinds, no curtains. The war surplus desk held a stained blotter, a telephone, a mayonnaise jar holding three pencils and two cheap ballpoint pens. R.J. Brooks & Associates was a no-frills operation.

Wanda Groz sat in a straight chair beside the desk, a steno pad balanced on her knee. She was good-looking in a boyish way, wore simple sexy clothes that R.J. liked. She had reddish hair cut in a modified pixie, wine-dark eyes, and an appealing overbite. Unmarried, she had a daughter living with her grandmother in Buffalo. She'd never explained the situation and R.J. had never asked. Every few months he found a reason to give her a bonus, knowing the extra money went directly to the child.

Wanda had been with him for three years and gave

no evidence of leaving. It was debatable who worked for whom. Still, it was an easy relationship and it worked for both of them.

R.J. munched on a jelly doughnut and sipped defensively at a cup of her coffee while dictating a final report for Tina Burkette.

"And so, in light of the enclosed photographic evidence, it seems unlikely that Mr. Burkette will reject any terms of settlement, no matter how high."

"Amen to that," muttered Wanda as she wrote.

"Paragraph. I therefore feel confident that if you instruct your lawyer accordingly, a settlement can be arrived at which is extremely advantageous to you. I hope I have proved etc., standard closing, send it registered mail."

As he dictated the last few sentences, he sealed the hot tub photograph in an envelope and put it into the evidence safe.

"I don't want to be standing too close," Wanda clucked, "when you get your just desserts."

R.J. gave her a grin and locked his hands behind his head, leaning so far back in his swivel chair he nearly disappeared below desk level.

"You think you're so smart, but I mean it," she said. "You're gonna be selling pencils on street corners."

"Mercantilism is the backbone of this nation's economy."

"So," she said finally, with a sigh, "are you going to tell me how you're involved in the Fontaine case?"

"No," he said.

"I saw her once, walking in the Village. She was even prettier than on the screen."

"She was a good-looking woman," R.J. agreed softly.

"Why would someone do a thing like that to a person like her?"

R.J. didn't have an answer.

"Well, are you going to call Kates? He's getting real testy. I don't think he's forgotten how stupid you made him look on the Boccarini case last year."

R.J. pulled a fresh cigar from the humidor and, getting up, stuffed it into his coat pocket. The room smelled of pipe tobacco and unlit cigars. He wouldn't allow smoking in the office; Wanda had to take her breaks in the ladies' room.

"On my way over there right now," he said.

"What about the lawyer?

"Said you got a letter?"

"On the front desk." She closed her pad and followed him into the cluttered reception room. "Just came this morning, hasn't even been date-stamped."

"Give it to me."

"It hasn't been logged."

"I'll log it, up here," he said, tapping his temple and reaching for his rain gear.

He turned as he shrugged on the coat, and froze. The *Post*, with a photograph of Belle Fontaine, was spread on Wanda's desk.

It was all there: Chubby-cheeked schoolgirl, blooming cheerleader and beauty contestant, fully ripened magazine and runway model, Hollywood starlet—and distinguished actress of stage and screen. A sidebar covered her sex life, including the controversial relationship with R.J.'s father.

"You got logs up there, all right," said Wanda, oblivious to his shock. She smoothed down her wraparound skirt. "I'm taking an early lunch, if that's all right with you. Do some shopping for the weekend."

"Trolling, you mean." He shook off the effect of the newspaper; what the hell did he care what they said?

Wanda stuck out her tongue.

"Bite that off one of these days," he told her, sticking

the letter in his coat pocket. He was glad she hadn't asked any more questions about the Fontaine case.

He'd already stepped into the elevator when Wanda called to him from the end of the hall. "Casey Wingate on the phone for you. Says it's important."

"I'll catch him later," he said. The elevator door slid shut.

———————————●———————————

He caught a cab out front and rode it to the precinct house. The driver's name was Akbar and he didn't speak much English, but he knew where the gas pedal was and R.J. stepped out of the cab at the precinct in record time.

A female officer with civilian hips led him across a reception area that looked like a bus station waiting room, up a flight of stairs, and to a door marked HOMICIDE. R.J. followed, watching the swing of those hips. *I must be feeling better,* he thought.

A dozen detectives, many of whom he knew, looked up from their files, newspapers, and crossword puzzles as he passed through the squad room. None of them had known his mother was Belle Fontaine. Now they all knew. He could feel the difference in the way they looked at him, sizing him up.

His escort left him at a glassed-in corner office where Lieutenant Kates waited with two men R.J. had never met.

"Detectives Angelo Bertelli and Don Boggs," Kates said without preamble. "R.J. Brooks."

They shook hands. Boggs, a heavyset guy in his early forties with a crewcut and a widow's peak that almost met his eyebrows, wore a shiny brown suit with grease spots on the lapels and the ugliest, square-bottom green knit tie R.J. had ever seen. He tried to squeeze the bones out of R.J.'s hand. But R.J. quickly shifted grip so it couldn't hurt, and Boggs gave up.

Bertelli gave him a firm, friendly handshake. He was maybe thirty, with carefully styled black hair. In spite of himself, R.J. warmed to the younger guy. He was not handsome, but he had a sparkle in his eyes that R.J. liked and knew women would go crazy for. He wore a tailored gray suit and a silk shirt.

"That's enough of the orgy," Kates snarled. "Sit down, Brooks."

Boggs sat in a hard-backed chair and Bertelli stepped back and perched on the windowsill.

"Or is it R.J. Fontaine?" Kates sneered.

R.J. looked at him. They'd had many heated confrontations. Kates played by the book and made that seem wrong. He'd never liked R.J., who would skate pretty close to the line in order to get a job done and had no use for somebody who liked the rules more than the game.

R.J. could tell that discovering his relationship with Belle Fontaine had not made Kates fall in love with him. If possible, Kates liked him even less now.

They'd never fought with more than words, but it had been close more than once. Fred Kates was a big man, Duke Wayne big. He was in his forties with brown eyes and florid cheeks. He brushed his thinning hair straight back. He wore a green three-piece suit that matched the peeling wall paint, with gold accessories on his wrists and fingers. He had snake eyes.

"What happened to your face?"

"Fraternity football game. You should see the other guys."

Only Bertelli laughed.

"Why haven't you come around before now?" Kates demanded.

"Why should I?"

"Should've known we'd be looking for you, once we tumbled to your tony bloodline."

R.J. shrugged. "I'm not that hard to find."

"You don't answer your home phone. Your secretary doesn't know where you are—what do you call that?"

R.J. nodded at Kates's two sidekicks. "They don't know their way around the neighborhood yet?"

Boggs snarled at him. "We look like rookies to you?"

"We're from Downtown, Homicide Division," Bertelli explained.

"Downtown, huh?" said R.J. "Sure, I get it. Pressure from upstairs—commissioner, mayor, governor? Media termites?"

You had to expect it in a celebrity case. The suits wanted action. Suspects. Arrests. Soundbites. Media trials and convictions. They wanted votes and they wanted administration appointments and they didn't really care if they got the real killer, so long as they could take a piece of red meat to the nightly news hounds.

"We'll ask the questions, Brooks." Kates reached for the cylinder from a .45 cleverly fashioned into a paperweight. "Where were you the night Belle Fontaine was killed?"

"What night was that?"

Kates thumped the desk with his paperweight. "You know goddamned well what night your mother was murdered," said Boggs. "Now where the hell were you?"

"On a job."

"What job? Where?"

"Surveillance. Over by the river."

"C'mon, Brooks," Boggs said, a threatening edge in his voice.

R.J. bristled. "C'mon yourself. You know damned well I'm not going to tell you a goddamned thing about my business without a warrant."

"Look," Bertelli said, "why not be reasonable?" He shifted his Italian loafers on the cigarette-scarred floor and leaned back against the windowsill. "You know we've got a job to do."

"Better make sure you do it right."

Lieutenant Kates pounded the desk with his fist, so hard the paperweight turned onto its side and rolled across the blotter like a toy drum. "I've put up with a lot of crap from you before, Brooks. But not this time. This time we play by the book."

R.J. jumped up. "Great. Then go by the book—get a warrant. I've had enough of this."

Boggs put a hand on his waist to restrain him. R.J. slapped the hand away.

"Jesus Christ." Boggs came out of his chair in a crouch. "Are you packing in here?"

"I've got a permit."

"He does," said Kates.

The two men glared at each other like a pair of cur dogs.

"Just watch yourself," Boggs breathed.

"I think maybe I'll watch you," R.J. replied.

Bertelli put an apologetic hand on his sleeve. "Look, R.J.—mind if I call you 'R.J.'? No? Good, listen. Why don't you cut us a little slack and we'll do the same for you." He spoke with the inflection of his old Bronx neighborhood, with an overlay of night-school polish. "Maybe we came on a little hard, but you're right, we are getting a lot of pressure on this one. You know what it's like. We're all a little uptight, that's all. Cut us a break here."

R.J. took a deep breath and leaned back in his chair. R.J. knew Bertelli was trying to manipulate him, but the guy was smooth and likable. Besides, he could always use a friend on the force.

So he might as well see what they were up to. Let them think he was taken in by their shopworn good guy–bad guy, Mutt and Jeff routine. Under different circumstances they were probably okay guys. Except Boggs, of course. And Kates—his was no act. R.J. had long ago pegged him as a dangerous coward.

"Okay," he told Bertelli. "Why didn't you say so in the first place? I just don't like to be hassled." He even managed a polite smile. "How can I help?"

"For starters, you can tell us the last time you saw your mother alive."

R.J. was stumped. "Jesus, I'm not sure."

"Last week, last month?" Boggs prompted.

"No, longer. Uh—hell. Ten months ago. Maybe eleven. I think."

He saw their reaction. They didn't believe he could live in the same galaxy as a mother like Belle Fontaine and never see her.

"Well, where were you the night she was killed, and who can verify it?" Bertelli asked. "We don't need to know the identity of your client right away."

R.J. thought about the prospect of using Burkette's bodyguard as an alibi witness. He laughed. Kates's face pulsed like an angry boil.

"This ain't getting us nowhere," he said. "Take him downstairs and reason with him. You don't get his cooperation we'll go to the nearest judge and get a warrant."

R.J. looked at Kates. "A warrant for what?"

"For your apartment, your office, and your rectal cavity before I'm through with you. Now get him outta here!"

CHAPTER 8

So you see how it is," said Bertelli, fanning his mouth as he moved a chunk of hot pizza from one cheek to the other. They had been discussing the case and the pressure on the investigators. *"Gesu!* Almost burned the tongue outa my mouth, that fuckin' cheese. Careful how you bite into that thing."

R.J. said, "You're different when you're on your own time."

"Sure, who isn't? You know. I use that college talk around Kates and his bunch of asshole-suckers. Keeps 'em off balance, makes 'em listen to me. I even red-pencil the Looie's grammar in his memos—drives him up the fuckin' wall."

They laughed, and R.J. began to relax. He looked around the crowded neighborhood tavern. Ippolito's. It looked like a place where a hit man walks in the back door and whacks a godfather all over his linguine and clam sauce. The rain had stopped, and the Bronx sidewalk swarmed with a late-lunch crowd.

"I been coming here since I was a kid," Bertelli said. "My uncle used to wait tables in the main dining room."

"Made a fortune on the ponies and retired to Miami Beach?" suggested R.J.

Bertelli shrugged. "Drowned when he was forty."

"Couldn't swim?"

"Not with a grand piano tied to his neck."

R.J. laughed. "You're a cop, and a wop, and a dandy, but you're okay. What do you want to hear from me? I didn't kill her."

The detective wiped his mouth with a linen napkin. "I didn't think you did."

Bertelli's nails were manicured, hair immaculately styled. Eyes and mouth a romance novelist would call sensual. Not handsome, but there was a kinetic aura about him.

"Kates and Boggs do," R.J. said, wondering how far he could be trusted.

"Boggs is an asshole," said Bertelli. "Wants people to think he's the strong silent type. You know, Dirty Harry. He's not, he's just stupid."

R.J. grinned sourly. "The lieutenant's not stupid."

"No, Fred's smart. And he's mean."

"And dirty?"

Bertelli's eyebrows shot up. "Whoa."

"Okay, let that go. But if you want me to cooperate, it's gotta work both ways. What've you guys come up with besides what's in the news?"

Bertelli sighed. "Not a hell of a lot, and that's a fact."

"Witnesses?"

"An old couple in the next room, deaf and dumb."

"Prints?"

"Plenty. Good ones too. Palms, feet, tits 'n' ass. Sorry, I don't mean to make light of this. But they all

match up with the victims—and a couple of our
schmucks working the crime scene. Nothing on a possible perp."

"Physical evidence?"

Bertelli shook his head. "That's the funny thing
about the crime scene. Too neat, too tidy for a murder.
It looked"—He gestured with his hands—"I don't
know. Like it was staged. Bodies arranged just so." He
shuddered. "Creepy. Anyway, no hairs, no fibers, no
shell casings. Nothing."

"No shell casings?"

Bertelli nodded. "What kind of guns you own?" he
asked. "We knew about that goddamn cannon you
carry. Got any other pieces around the office?"

"Old army .45, couple .22s, and a .38 Smith & Wes-
son. All legal and accounted for. What'd the shooter
use?"

"I shouldn't be talking so much. A .38."

"Guess that does make me a suspect."

"Aw, you know. Not really, but it's neater if we can
check out your piece."

"Well, I don't know. No offense, but I don't think I
want your co-workers parading through my office and
fooling with my guns. They might shoot my secretary."

"We can get a warrant."

"Sure, Kates would love to have an excuse to open
up my files."

"I'm not Lieutenant Kates, R.J. And I don't wanna
open your files. I just want to catch a killer."

R.J. started to speak, but Bertelli raised a finger and
smiled, gave his head a half shake to show he wasn't
done talking yet. "Now, I'm a cop, R.J. I gotta play by
the rules, least as long as the Looie is breathin' down
my neck. I know you didn't kill anybody, and it's a
waste of time chasing after you like you did.

"So what I gotta do is cross you off the lieutenant's

list as quick as possible, *capish*? And that way I can knock off alla this *stronzo* and get down to catching whoever did this thing. We on the same level here?"

R.J. almost had to laugh. The guy was so smooth and sincere, with those deep brown eyes. He'd go far in the Department, if R.J. was any judge.

"All right, Jesus. You should sell time-share condos, Angelo. Just say when, I'll tell my girl at the office to turn it over."

Bertelli smiled. "Thanks, man. I mean that."

"That's what good citizens are for."

They finished their pizza and Bertelli ordered another beer. R.J. was drinking coffee. When the waitress left, she smiled at Bertelli and smoothed her uniform over her hips as if it were a sequined gown.

"Jesus Christ," said R.J. "How do you *do* that?"

Bertelli shrugged it off with one of those Italian vowel sounds that mean so much. "Ehh," he said. "You know, your mother was really something. I seen every picture she ever made. And I saw her on Broadway three years ago in that musical. Man . . . She was really . . ." He trickled to a stop, his olive complexion flushing with embarassment.

"It was the legs," R.J. said.

"What about your stepfather? What was their relationship after the divorce?"

"They were only together a couple of years. I haven't seen him in a long time."

"Not since you went off to college."

R.J. gave him a look. "You know a lot about me."

Bertelli shrugged. "I been boning up. Truth is, I've been looking forward to meeting you since Kates put me on the case. You got quite a reputation."

"Don't believe everything the cops tell you."

"You went to law school," Bertelli said.

"No degree. I was expelled for cheating."

"I know. Cheating with the dean's wife."

They laughed together.

"Hey, why are you doing this marital proctology. You know people, you could do a lot of business with the Hollywood crowd. Even right here on Broadway."

"Not my cup of hemlock."

"What about TV? Ever met a producer named Casey Wingate?"

R.J. hesitated. "Wingate?" He shrugged. "I never heard of him."

He could tell Bertelli wasn't convinced, but the detective didn't push it. Which left R.J. wondering just what he had in mind and how Casey Wingate figured into it. When he got back to his office he'd have Wanda run a quick backgrounder on the producer.

"He the sporting type, your stepfather? You know, guns, shooting?"

R.J. was jostled by the quick shift in focus; he frowned over long-abandoned memories. "He hunts birds down south somewhere, bigger game out west. That's all I know. More than I want to know."

Bertelli pondered his next question. "Think he could have killed your mother?"

R.J. was ready for it. "Sure. Anybody can kill, given the right circumstances. Or the wrong ones."

"You think he did it?"

"No."

"Neither do I."

"You go at your work by elimination. Ever catch anybody?"

The detective smiled. "Helps to know who didn't do it."

R.J. sipped some coffee. "Okay, Angelo. Now tell me, why is Kates so determined to pin my mother's death on me?"

Bertelli shook his head. "I don't think he much likes you, R.J."

R.J. laughed. "No shit."

"Besides, you got the best motive. A few million smackeroos ain't small antipasto."

"What the hell are you talking about?"

Bertelli looked at him like he was stupid. He was starting to feel like maybe he was.

"You really don't know? How close were you to your mother?"

The question stung, and it showed. "What does that have to do with anything?"

"She left everything to you, bucko. At least that's the way I see it. No brothers or sisters, your father's long dead, she was divorced from your stepfather. No companions we know about. I haven't seen the will, of course. Haven't you talked to Jackson Yates?"

"How do you know about him?"

"Called us the morning after your mother was murdered. She'd been working on a TV piece about her career with that producer, Casey Wingate. Yates was handling the legal aspects."

R.J. remembered the letter from the lawyer and fished it out of his pocket.

"Read it," said Bertelli. "I'll get us some more coffee."

CHAPTER 9

Bertelli dropped him off at an address on West 33rd Street. "I'll send somebody for your piece, R.J.," he said as R.J. opened the door. Then Bertelli winked. "Or do I gotta call you 'Mr. Brooks,' now you're rich?"

"Knock it off, Angelo," R.J. said. He was in no mood for that sort of kidding. "Talk to you later," he said, and he slid out of the car.

Bertelli chuckled as he pulled away into traffic.

The building was a massive turn-of-the century thing with gingerbread all over the outside. Large gold letters on the door said INDEPENDENT PRODUCTIONS, INC.

The lobby was deserted except for a uniformed guard with a bank of telephones and a closed-circuit TV monitor behind his desk. He gave R.J.'s bruised face a suspicious look but called upstairs on the strength of his business card.

R.J. rode up in the elevator alone, pondering the contents of the letter from Jackson Yates. His mother had named R.J. the executor of her estate. And Bertelli had guessed right: He was also the primary beneficiary. According to Yates it was up to R.J. to settle all probate matters as expeditiously as possible. R.J. had phoned him from the restaurant and made an appointment for the following afternoon.

Upstairs, R.J. stepped out into a floorplan that resembled the shell of an uncompleted warehouse. The shooting studio was in the center, bound by corridors on three sides that serviced a warren of cluttered cubbyholes. The dress code favored jeans and sweaters, loafers and desert boots. The on-camera people were the only ones who dressed for the public.

A girl wearing an oversized sweater and glasses led him to an office with a hand-lettered sign on the door: CASEY WINGATE.

An attractive young woman stood in the middle of the room flipping through a file, a pencil clamped between her teeth. Her auburn hair framed a face that was both sensual and hard-edged, a face that said Private School, Smart and Ambitious. She looked up at him and raised a perfect eyebrow.

"Sorry," he said. "I'm looking for Casey Wingate."

"I'm Wingate."

"Say what?"

She slid the pencil out of her mouth and into a mass of hair, notching it behind her ear. "I'm Casey Wingate." She looked him over, taking in the bruised face and battered trench coat with a slight smile. "And I know who you are, Mr. Brooks."

"Well," he said, sliding the business card back into his coat pocket, "I'll be damned."

"You may well be."

He had the feeling she didn't like him much. "You called my office this morning," he said.

"And yesterday, and the day before."

"I've been out."

She gave him a scornful half-smile and closed the file. R.J. watched as she went to her desk. Probably taller than him in high heels. But today she wore sensible flats with a knee-length wool skirt. She was, he suspected, routinely looked at by men in restaurants, whistled at by hardhats on the sidewalk. A woman used to male attention and not bothered by it.

No wedding or engagement ring, but that didn't mean much these days. Nails long and tapered, painted with clear polish. He liked that.

"Take off your coat. Sit down," she said, and then her manner softened. "I'm sorry about your mother. I didn't know her well, but I liked her. I think we might have become friends."

"I didn't even know she was in town."

"There's a lot you didn't know about her."

"What's that supposed to mean?"

She ignored the question. "I know why you're here. The tapes. I've been looking for you because you play a role in the piece I've been working on. We need to understand each other."

"You don't beat around the bush."

She looked at her watch. "And I don't like to waste time."

"Fair enough. Your tapes might answer some crucial questions about my mother's death. I need anything you've got about her last few weeks. When did she come here? Why? Where did she go? Who did she see? What were her plans?"

"The sort of things most sons might already know about their mothers."

His eyes narrowed. "Don't think you've got me figured out too easily, Wingate."

She sat on a corner of the desk, pressing the file against her chest and swinging her foot. "Oh, I think I understand you, Mr. Brooks. For a public figure, Belle was amazingly candid, and my research has been as thorough as time and money permit. But I'm always ready to learn more. And I'm willing to be proved wrong."

He sat forward on the edge of his chair. "Then let's get to work. When can I see some film?"

"I'm not sure you can."

"Meaning?"

"Meaning I've made a deal with the studio. They were financing the project. My boss might object."

"Then get him in here. Who is he, what's his name?"

A man's nasal voice said, "Pike. His name is Colin Pike."

R.J. turned to find a lump of dough standing in the doorway wearing a pair of white jeans and a USC sweatshirt.

"My boss," said Casey Wingate. R.J. got the impression she was not too happy about the situation. He knew one thing at a glance, though: They weren't involved, as the saying goes. For some reason, he was glad.

"I know what you want, and you can't have them," Pike said, like a petulant child. R.J. stood up and Pike held his ground. "The police have already been here, asking for them. I told them to come back with a warrant. I'm telling you the same thing."

"You bastard. Those tapes might help solve a murder."

"What do you care? From what I hear you didn't even like her."

R.J. clenched his fist, and Casey stepped between them. But Pike had already scuttled into the hall and summoned a nearby security guard. "Put this guy outta here," he told the guard, a muscular black man. "And I want you in my office *now,* Wingate."

Pike rolled back along the hall like an underdone muffin on skates. Casey went with R.J. and the guard to the elevator.

"It's been . . . interesting," she said.

They didn't shake hands; they didn't need to. When she had brushed past him to stop him from decking Pike, accidentally touching him, he had felt a jolt of electricity. He could see she was feeling it too, even without physical contact.

"I'll see you again," he told her, tossing his coat over his shoulder.

"Count on it," she said.

The elevator door slid shut between them.

R.J. let out a long breath. So did the guard. "You lucky, mister. You got out without being skinned alive. That woman is one tough honky."

R.J. grinned. "You can play that again, Sam."

"Say what?" said the guard.

"Skip it."

CHAPTER 10

There were a lot of Wingates in the Manhattan book.
There was no listing for a Casey but R.J. found a K.C.
Wingate on Houston Street in the Village. Close
enough, he thought. Probably hates the name Katherine. It had to be Katherine.

Just to be sure he called the receptionist at Independent Productions. "Hi, this is personnel services," he
said in a light and breezy voice. "We're updating the
files. Can you confirm the current home address of
your K.C. Wingate? At 159 Houston Street?"

"One moment please," the cool British voice said. A
moment later the Muzak clicked off and the Brit said,
"That is the correct address."

"Thanks. Bye!" said R.J. and hung up.

He figured she was the type to work late, but he'd
been wrong before. So he had her doorway staked out
by four o'clock. At eight-thirty he was still there.

He'd been propositioned three times, twice by men

and once by a woman who should have been working
the docks, with her tiny tube top and tight black skirt.
She looked almost blue in the cold, so thin a good wind
would blow her across the river to Jersey.

He'd seen eleven people walking dogs. Thirty-two
kids went by, nineteen of them with a parent or nanny.

One time, at about a quarter of eight, a drunk
stepped into the doorway where R.J. was standing. The
man unzipped his fly before he saw R.J. Then he stood
there with his hand in his pants, blinking stupidly.

"Sorry," R.J. told him. "This stall is in use."

The drunk staggered backward and disappeared
down the sidewalk, hand still in his pants.

R.J. sympathized with the man. He had to pee so
bad his ears were ringing, and he was about to give up
the whole thing as a bad idea at a quarter to nine, when
a taxi stopped in front of her door and Casey got out.
As she paid the driver, R.J. crossed the street and
stepped over beside her.

"Where in hell have you been?" he asked her.

She gave a little jump, then turned to face him.
"Looking for you," she said coolly.

R.J. was startled, but he believed she was telling the
truth and not just smart-mouthing him. This woman
had a lot of moxie.

The cab pulled away and Casey looked him in the
eye. "Well?" she said.

"Well, what?"

"Well, what did you have in mind?"

A raindrop hit R.J.'s forehead. He glanced up.
There were plenty more where that one came from.
"Listen, can we talk someplace? This is about to get a
little wetter than I like it." He meant the rain, but if he
didn't find a bathroom soon it would be even wetter.

She looked at him hard for a moment. "All right.
Come on up." She turned toward the door, pulling a

large key ring out of her shoulder bag.

Casey's apartment was on the third floor at the back. It had a lot of space for a New York apartment, but not much view. R.J. could just make out a warehouse about eight feet away through the only window he could see.

There were a couple of very nice prints on the wall; a little too modern for R.J.'s taste, but good stuff.

He got Casey's permission to use her bathroom, and he barely managed not to run down the short hall. He came back feeling a great deal better.

"What do you want to talk about?" she asked him.

R.J. looked over the sparsely furnished open room. A few small rugs were scattered on the hardwood floor, and there was a large bookcase with very few open spaces on it.

"Were you really looking for me?"

"I said I was."

R.J. spotted a canvas-backed director's chair and sank into it. "Why?"

Casey tossed her shoulder bag onto a low black couch with a steel frame and started to shrug out of her raincoat. "Same reason you were looking for me, I'm sure."

"Sure, I like that. And what would that be?"

She blew out a long breath and planted herself in front of him. "Can we cut the crap, Brooks? I've got something you want, and I want something from you too. That's a pretty good starting place. Instead of dicking around, we could be working it out already."

R.J. had never liked aggressive women, but he was ready to make an exception. "What did you have in mind?"

She moved over and hung herself on the couch, smoothing her skirt down over her long legs. The sharp angle of the couch showed them off to real advantage.

"The piece I was doing on your mother. It's more important than ever now. And just so all my cards are on the table, I am not exaggerating when I say this story could really make my career. So you know what's in it for me, okay? It's a very hot story."

"Nothing like a little murder to raise interest in a fading star."

She looked annoyed, but she went on. "The fact is, she was in the middle of a comeback. I think my piece would have helped. About halfway through, I realized I *wanted* it to help." Casey gave him a very small smile. "I guess I lost my objectivity. I liked your mother. She was very easy to talk to."

"Not for me."

"Maybe you never gave her a chance."

"Yeah. That must have been it. Maybe I should have opened up to her, in between the boarding schools and the summer camps, and really let her into my life in the three days a year she could put up with me. We could have had some great talks, maybe for the full five minutes at a time she could focus on something besides her career. I should have tried harder. I feel like a jerk."

He was surprised at how the words all came out like that. Casey really knew how to get to him, and she had.

She looked at him without blinking for a long minute. He couldn't read her expression. "I'm sorry you feel that way," she said finally.

"Sweetheart, so am I."

"People change, you know."

"I know, I've done it myself."

"It may be that your mother hit a certain age and looked back and didn't like what she saw. She might have been trying to reach out to you."

"She had a funny way of reaching out. I didn't even know she was in town. Maybe if I had a press card, she would have sent a release, let me know she was coming."

Casey gave him that long stare again, the one he couldn't read. Finally she shook her head. "She's dead, R.J. Can't you like her even a little bit?"

"No, I can't," he snarled. He got up and stepped over to the couch, glaring down at her. "I can't like her at all. Not that it's any of your business. I never could like her. Only a camera could like that woman. But I loved her. She was my mother. I loved *her*—not some character she played, and not a sob sister attitude she was trying out on some soggy reporter. I loved my mother, Miss Wingate, and I am mad as hell that she's gone, and that somebody killed her like that, and whoever it is I'm going to find them, and I may or may not turn 'em over to the cops when I do, all right? Now quit fishing for a story and show me the goddamn tapes before you have me chewing up your furniture."

Something finally showed in her eyes. Approval? Amusement? He couldn't tell. "All right, R.J.," she said and stood up smoothly. "Just so we understand each other. You're after a killer, I'm after a story. I'll show you the tapes—but you've got to help me out too. Deal?"

She held out a hand. He looked at her, and the elegant hand, for a long moment. Then he laughed.

"What the hell," he said. "Deal." He took her hand. The electricity was still there, maybe stronger. Casey pulled her hand back with a slightly startled look.

"Good," she said, already smoothing over any sign that she had felt anything she didn't want to feel. "Do you have any ideas yet about the murder?"

He shook his head. "Not a clue. I guess it could be one of those star stalker things—but it could be a lot of other things too. She was no angel, and she stepped hard on a lot of people."

"So you think it was someone from her past?"

R.J. shook his head. "I didn't say that. But it could have been, sure. Something's been bothering me, something I saw on a piece of your film."

"What was it?"

R.J. turned away. The view out the window hadn't changed. "I don't know. It's not even a hunch yet. Just—something doesn't look quite right. I can't tell you any more."

"Can't—or won't?" There was a cool challenge in her voice. He turned back to face her.

"Why don't we look at the tapes, and I'll let you know?"

She studied him briefly, then nodded. "All right. I have them right here." She pulled open her shoulder bag and took out four plain videocassettes.

Casey crossed to the far side of the room and R.J. followed. She had a twenty-seven-inch Sony monitor set up there and a rack of VTRs: two three-quarter-inch, one VHS, even a Beta. There was a joystick editing panel mounted on a small counter, two smaller monitors, and some other equipment for film as well as video.

"Quite a setup," R.J. said.

She shrugged. "Not really. It's kind of primitive. But it lets me do some of the rough cuts here, without that asshole Pike reaching for my knee in the dark editing bay."

R.J. snorted. "Should've known he was a knee-grabber. Few more years, he'll probably be a Shriner."

She put in the first tape and started to rewind it.

"You haven't told me yet what you think about my mother's murder."

She didn't look up. "I don't think it was a mob hit or anything like that. Too pretty. And I don't think it was a jealous wife, for the same reason."

"Pretty?" R.J. snarled. "What the hell was pretty about it?"

The tape made a snapping sound and popped out of the machine. She pushed it back in. "Have you seen pictures of the crime scene?" She didn't wait for an answer. "Whoever it was didn't just come in, shoot them, and go out. Whoever did this, they spent a lot of time composing the picture they would leave behind. I've been in this business awhile, and I can tell a pro at work when I see one. This guy was a pro."

"What, you mean a pro killer?"

She shook her head. "I mean show business," she said. R.J. blinked hard as she went on. "Everything was just so, just like somebody was setting up models for a picture. A very startling and unusual picture." Now she looked up at him. "That's why I brought these other tapes."

"Why?"

"Because in the last eighteen months there have been other unsolved murders where the crime scene was arranged the same way."

R.J. felt for his cigar and stuck it into his face. He bit down hard. "Do the cops know about this?"

Her eyes gleamed. "They have the same information I have, R.J."

He barked out a short laugh. "But they don't have your brains, right? You're okay, kid." He sank into the other chair beside her. "All right. Let's take a look."

Casey leaned forward and grabbed the joystick. "This is the first one," she said, leaning the stick forward. She wound quickly past some standard-looking interview footage, a few exterior shots, and then: "There." She stopped the tape.

The camera was looking down on the back of a nude body, male, middle-aged. The guy would never have made anybody's pin-up calendar alive, and dead he was far beyond a little unsightly.

A pool of blood spread out around the body, although no marks were visible on the man's back.

Just out of reach of his outstretched hand was a battered ukulele.

R.J. frowned and leaned closer. "What's that?" He pointed at the screen. Something was barely visible, tucked in between the cheeks of the body's naked buttocks.

Casey gave him a grimace. "It's a spread of pictures. Polaroids. Cops wouldn't let me see 'em. Said they were too gruesome."

"Jesus." He shook his head. "Cause of death?"

She was already rewinding the second tape. "The closest they could come was to say either shock from multiple injuries or loss of blood. They said it looked like some kind of crazy surgery, where the doctor didn't really know what he was looking for, but he kept looking anyway."

She stopped and once again ran the tape ahead with the joystick. The same kind of stuff: same crime-scene crew. Then she stopped the tape again. "Number two."

There was a woman wired to a straight-backed chair. At least, R.J. was pretty sure it had been a woman. It looked like her lips, and most of her face, had been eaten away by acid. In her hand was a cheap Japanese fan.

"Were there Polaroids at this one?"

Casey nodded and hit rewind. "At all of them. But the police—it was a Lieutenant Kates in particular, do you know him?"

R.J. nodded. His lips moved away from his teeth, but it wasn't a smile. "I know Freddy."

"Well, he felt that the way each victim was killed was

so different they couldn't be connected. The Polaroids had to be coincidence."

"He also feels he doesn't want the blowdries from the evening news on his ass about a serial killer," said R.J. "But maybe he's right. What makes you think they *are* connected?"

She looked him square in the eye. "When I was a freshman in college the girls on my floor played a game. It was called Date Lit 101. The others would pick a character from fiction and you had to tell what a first date with that character would be like."

"Who did you get?" he asked her with a wolfish grin.

"Stephen Dedalus, from *Portrait of the Artist as a Young Man.*"

"Sounds like a pretty dull date."

"The point is, you had to get inside the head of these characters, the books. It was always you, but the experience was different.

"That's what the killer is doing."

R.J. blinked. "I must have missed something there."

She sighed at him impatiently. "You had to *think* like the character, then set up a date the way he would have done it. The killer is doing the same thing. He's committing each murder like he's playing a different part—a different *character* is committing each murder, but it's the same actor, don't you see?"

R.J. whistled. No wonder Kates was skeptical. "I guess I don't. How can you tell?"

She shrugged. "At the moment, it's just a feeling I've got," she said, and then seeing his expression she added, "What, you never get hunches?"

"I've got one right now. Roll that tape forward."

She turned and pushed the joystick again. "What are you looking for?"

"Footage of the funeral, if you have it. I thought—there!"

She stopped the tape. A small crowd was gathered at an open grave. "Okay, run it forward, slowly." The tape went on, frame by frame. "Stop." Casey froze it and R.J. leaned forward.

An overweight man with a florid complexion was leaning on an adjacent tombstone, looking just a little tipsy somehow. It was hard to make out too many details of his face, but R.J. was sure he'd never seen the man before. Except—

"Next tape." Again they wound forward to the funeral. And once again R.J. stopped it as the camera panned across a solitary man on the outskirts of the small crowd. "Stop."

She shook her head. "This guy's a lot skinnier."

"So he was wearing padding before. Look at the face."

This time he was a Jesuit priest, looking solemnly toward the grave. He was about the same height as the drunk, but slimmer. R.J. couldn't quite make out the face. The angle was bad and the cameraman wasn't really focusing on the priest. But it could have been the same face, or at least similar, as though the two men were related.

More than that, though, was—what? Something he could not for the life of him put his finger on.

He swore softly under his breath.

"What? Do you see something?" Casey asked, frowning at the monitor.

"I don't know. It's hard to be sure. But after what you said about one guy playing different parts, and the feeling I already got about this . . . I don't know." He shook his head. It was just too stupid to say out loud.

Casey leaned toward him impatiently. "Come on,

R.J., don't hold out on me. What've you got?"

He threw the mangled cigar at the wastebasket and let the breath hiss out between his teeth. "I think I recognize the actor," he said.

CHAPTER **11**

R.J. was unable to shake that haunting feeling of familiarity. He and Casey had looked at the tapes over and over until almost dawn, and when he finally stumbled down the stairs to go home all they could agree on was that it might be the same guy.

But the name wouldn't come, and he could not remember how or why the face was familiar.

R.J. took the subway home, hoping the adrenaline rush of danger would keep him awake. But all the muggers must have taken the night off too, and he dozed around Grand Central Station. He woke up one stop past his and walked back.

The elevator was out again in his building, so he climbed the four flights up to his apartment, so tired he couldn't even think of a good death threat for the super.

He opened the door and stood blinking for a good thirty seconds, sure he was hallucinating.

There was a body on his couch.

"Shit," he said, and the body sat up.

"Well," said Henry Portillo, stretching. "Hell of a time to be tomcatting around, R.J. Your mother's funeral is this afternoon."

R.J. was stung. "It's all right for *you* to sleep," he snapped. "She was my mother."

Portillo froze in midyawn. R.J. could see the remark had hurt. Tough, he thought.

"All right, R.J.," he said softly, "let's just start over, okay? Where have you been all night?"

"Working. With that TV producer, Casey Wingate."

Portillo nodded. "What did you find?"

R.J. sank into a chair and rubbed his bleary eyes. "I'm not sure if I found anything. But I think we got a serial killer. I don't know how or why he got on to my mother. Maybe coincidence. And—"

He hesitated. He knew that Uncle Hank, like most long-time cops, would respect a hunch. But it was still tough to put into words something that indefinite. Still, he wanted the older man's input. "I think I know the guy."

Hank leaned forward, his eyes gleaming. "Tell me," he demanded.

R.J. ran it all down for him: the different figures at the funerals that *could* have been the same man in different disguises, Casey's ideas about the role-playing, the haunting feeling that he knew that face. When he finished, Hank lounged back on the couch, his brow furrowed in thought.

"It fits," he said. "When I saw what the crime scene was like . . ." He shook his head. "A one-time killer, somebody who does it for revenge, out of passion, whatever—somebody like that doesn't do those things. This guy took a lot of time, made it look perfect."

"He'll be there this afternoon," R.J. said.

"That fits too," Portillo agreed. "Let's see if we can't catch him. But first . . ." He stood up. "It has been, by my account, almost three years since you have had a proper breakfast."

"Uncle Hank—"

But Portillo held up a hand to cut him off. "No, R.J. You are tired, and you're hungry. You can't catch a killer without a fire in your belly, and I'm going to put it there." With that he headed for the kitchen.

R.J. trailed after him. "You can't even get most of the stuff you need in Manhattan," he protested.

"I brought it with me," answered Portillo, rummaging through several grocery bags. "Why don't you make coffee while I cook?"

In a very few minutes the two were sitting at the rickety kitchen table, tearing into *huevos rancheros* smothered in hot salsa, refried beans, and fresh, hot tortillas.

R.J. was surprised at how hungry he was. He wolfed down two full plates before settling back with his coffee.

"Better, huh?"

R.J. had to agree.

As R.J. stood up to get more coffee, there was a knock at the door.

Hank looked at him with a raised eyebrow, but R.J. shrugged. "Not a clue," he said and went to open the door.

Hookshot stood in the hall. R.J. gaped in surprise: His friend was wearing a tie with his black silk jacket. R.J. hadn't even known Hookshot owned a tie.

"R.J.," said Hookshot with grave formality, "is there anything you need? Anything I can do for you?"

"Yeah, there is," said R.J., holding wide the door. "Come on in."

The three of them sat in the kitchen with mugs of coffee. When they had filled Hookshot in, he nodded.

"Count me in. I can get some of the minimensch to help too." Hookshot had a small army of preteen boys working for him. They hawked papers, carried messages, and gathered information.

"All right," R.J. said. "The service is at Parker and McDonald's on 44th Street. It's not a big place. Should be easy enough to keep an eye out."

"Don't be so sure," said Hookshot. "This is going to be a circus. You'll have two or three hundred people from the press, God knows how many geeks and gawkers and goons. People be coming from everywhere, man."

"He's right," said Portillo.

"Sure, I know. But if they come in they all have to come through the door. I can keep an eye out—"

"Leave it to me," Hookshot said. "You're gonna be busy."

"I can handle it," R.J. said through his teeth.

"*Chico,* no. There is enough for you to do," Hank said.

"Hey," added Hookshot gently, "the news hounds be on your ass like slick on a pimp. Let the minimensch handle this, R.J. Kinda thing they good at."

"He is right," said Portillo. "Let him do it, him and his *pobrecitos.* You and I will be busy."

"You? What are you going to be doing?"

Uncle Hank looked at him with quiet hurt in his eyes. "I will be with you, *chico. Como siempre.*"

R.J. nodded, ashamed. "Like always."

"Be easy on this, R.J.," Hookshot told him. "I'll have a couple of little dudes on Rollerblades waiting outside. Midtown traffic like it's gonna be, they be faster than anyone on foot or in a car."

"All right," said R.J., suddenly overwhelmingly tired.

"So tell me again what we're looking for," Hookshot

said. " 'Could be anybody' just doesn't cut it."

"It's what we got," answered R.J.

"If this guy fits the kind of profile I think he does," Portillo tossed in, "he'll want to get close, be part of it. I think a guy like this, he will get off on being in your face without you knowing who he is."

"From what I figured out with Wingate," R.J. said, "he could look like just about anybody. Young, old, fat, thin—whatever he wants. But I agree with Uncle Hank: He'll want to get close."

Hookshot shook his head. "That's gonna fit just about everybody in town too. You don't know how they're talking about this on the street. You were selling tickets, you could retire tomorrow."

"All I can say is, keep an eye out for anybody who doesn't look quite right," said R.J.

"Or somebody who looks a little *too* right," Portillo added.

Hookshot nodded. "That should cover just about everybody," he said with a straight face. "Okay, I got a couple of real smart guys I can stick inside. You have to fix it for them, R.J."

"Can do," R.J. said.

Parker and McDonald's Funeral Home sat on 44th Street just two blocks off Times Square. For over a hundred years they had taken care of show people. Belle had specified them in her will, but she hadn't needed to. R.J. knew who they were. So did everybody.

They knew how to handle crowds too, but this crowd was pushing them to their limit.

R.J. took a cab over to the funeral home. Henry Portillo and Hookshot rode with him. The cabbie stopped three blocks away and told them, in his heavily accented English, that he couldn't get any closer and the gentlemen might want to walk the rest of the way.

But R.J. had only one foot out the cab door when the first of the news hounds hit him like a greasy squall. Within two steps he was in the eye of a hurricane.

He could see nothing but a forest of arms waving at him as if in a high wind. He could only hear his name shouted at him from a hundred mouths and snatches of self-important monologue blurted into microphones. "Sole heir and leading suspect" seemed to be one of the catchphrases, almost as if somebody had handed out a tear sheet with those words on it.

Portillo and Hookshot formed a barricade in front of him, and the three of them pushed their way through. Hands clutching microphones still blew in at R.J. from over their linked arms.

"Mr. Brooks! Is it true—"

"How did you feel—"

"What is your response to—"

"Mr. Brooks—"

"What was it like—"

"How did you *feel*—"

"Did you really—"

"The police say—"

With a block to go he'd had enough. He stopped walking and held up a hand for quiet. "Ladies and gentlemen! Please, just a moment, ladies and gentlemen!"

They didn't exactly get quiet, but they got quieter. When R.J. felt that all eyes were on him, he took a breath and looked squarely into the nearest camera. "Blow it out your asses," he said and turned to go.

He heard Hookshot snort out a short laugh, and Portillo whispered, "Feel a little better, *chico*?" And to his surprise, R.J. *did* feel a little better.

The feeling didn't last. Soon they were inside the funeral home. The smell turned R.J.'s stomach into a roiling knot. There was no mistaking it, that death smell, the sickly-sweet chemicals. He'd smelled it before, but this time it was too close, too personal.

His mother.

The dark, wood-paneled hall seemed to funnel the smell, the soft music, the feeling of death, and bring it straight into his gut with a hard, sharp jab.

He was conscious of Portillo beside him; Hookshot had slipped away to work the crowd, talk to his boys. But Hank stayed with him as the service droned on.

R.J. found that he couldn't hear the words of the service, just the tone of voice: monotonous, cloying, deeply regretful without any real emotion. It was being played for the cameras.

And cameras there were. About two-thirds of the mourners were media coyotes. At the back of the room he saw Casey Wingate. She was sitting quietly, dressed in a dignified dark wool suit that still managed to show off her legs. He assumed that at least one of the cameramen at the back was working for her, but Casey herself looked more like a mourner than a coyote. Her stock went up with R.J.

He made it through the service without strangling any reporters.

As they headed out for the rented limo now parked at the curb—all part of Parker and McDonald's star package—he saw Hookshot standing beside the door. They locked eyes; Hookshot gave his head one half-shake. Nothing.

He and Portillo shoved their way out the door to the limo. A howl went up from the reporters, like a pack of hounds baying at the moon.

One or two got close enough to shove a microphone at him and shout a question.

One of these was a very average-looking man in a careful suit and styled blond hair. On his dark suitcoat was a lapel tag that read "CABLE INDEPENDENT NEWS."

The man brutally elbowed a cluster of reporters out of the way and put his microphone right under R.J.'s nose.

"Mr. Brooks," he shouted, "how does it feel—"

But R.J. ignored him, just like all the others, and crawled into the limo with Portillo.

CHAPTER 12

R.J. moved numbly through the service at graveside. He was mildly surprised that it was hitting him so hard, but there wasn't much he could do about it.

When it was over, a rising tide of reporters shoved him back to the limo. He hadn't given them their soundbite yet, and they were starting to turn mean. But he made it into the backseat of the big Caddie, and as soon as he was joined by Hank and Hookshot, he signaled the driver to get going.

They drove in silence for about five minutes. Then Hookshot cleared his throat.

R.J. looked at his friend.

"None of my people saw doodle-squat, R.J.," he said. "Sorry." He shrugged. "Maybe he didn't show."

R.J. nodded. "He showed. He was there. I could feel him. I just couldn't find him."

Uncle Hank put a hand on his shoulder. "We may have been asking too much of ourselves, to stay alert on such an occasion." He shook his head sadly. "She was—your mother," he said. And R.J. wondered what the man had been thinking of saying in that tiny hesitation.

"What now, R.J.?" Hookshot asked.

R.J. looked out the window. It was a bright, warm afternoon. He felt like sleet should be coming down in cold sheets of misery.

"I don't know," he said. "I need a little time. I have to go through her stuff."

Again he felt Hank's hand on his shoulder; not hard, just a gentle pressure to say *I'm here.*

"I must get back to Quantico," Portillo said. "But I will be back on the weekend. And I may have something we can use."

R.J. looked up. He felt like he should be taking charge of finding the killer, pointing Portillo and Hookshot down likely paths, but he couldn't focus enough.

"What do they have in Quantico that we might want?" he asked.

Henry placed a blunt brown finger against his forehead. "The BSU—Behavioral Science Unit. They have a program I can use to work up a profile of the killer."

"You believe that shit?" asked Hookshot. He raised one scarred eyebrow halfway up to his hairline.

He nodded. "I do. The Bureau has been having very good results finding serial killers with this workup. I think it can help us."

"Uh-huh," Hookshot said. He didn't sound convinced.

⬤

They dropped R.J. at Central Park West and 79th and he walked to his mother's apartment.

The building was not on everybody's list of top ten

celebrity apartment buildings, and Belle had preferred it that way. Nonetheless, it was a beautiful old building, with a great view of the Park, and very secure.

The uniformed doorman was an ex-cop who packed a piece he wasn't afraid to use. He knew R.J., although there hadn't been that many visits.

"Morning, Mr. Brooks," he said, touching his cap.

"Hey, Tony," said R.J.

"Sorry about your mom. She was a grand lady."

"Yeah, thanks. Uh—I guess I have to go through her stuff."

The doorman nodded and reached into his pocket. "I been expecting youse," he said. He placed a key in R.J.'s hand. "You know where it is," he said, with a touch of—was it disapproval? That R.J. hadn't been a more dutiful son? He probably thinks I should have come every week for Sunday dinner, R.J. thought dourly.

"Yeah, I know where it is, Tony," said R.J., a little harder than he had to.

Tony shrugged. "I guess the place is yours now."

R.J. nodded and thought, What the hell. He put a fiver in Tony's hand.

"I guess it is. Thanks for the key."

"Forget about it," said Tony.

The elevator let him off on the seventh floor and he let himself into the apartment.

And then he just stood and looked around.

How did you do that? Go through her stuff? Where did you start? What did you look for?

Her stuff. The apartment was furnished sparely but elegantly. So very much like her.

No designer had been here. This place had been *hers*, and the things in it were for her comfort.

And it had not been entirely his fault that he had been here so rarely. She did not like other people in this place. Although she was very social when the mood was on her, she did not socialize here. It was her Fortress of Solitude, and she was extremely fussy about who she let in.

R.J. took a deep breath. The place even smelled like her. Well, he thought, gotta start somewhere.

He moved through the rooms: living room, bedroom. He peeked into the bathroom. Back to the living room, the kitchen. The spare bedroom, which she called her office.

He sat in the high-backed swivel chair at his mother's desk. It was a rolltop, a beautiful piece of furniture.

The top of the desk was neat. There was a clean blotter, a pencil holder, a stapler, a small calculator—the kind with the roll of paper to print out your figures.

At the back of the desk were a row of small drawers, tiny pigeonholes, and some vertical slots for storing correspondence. R.J. riffled through the envelopes standing in these. Mostly bills, bank and broker statements. There was a stack of unused envelopes, the kind with the stamp already on.

He opened the largest drawer, the one in the center.

Inside sat a stack of old-looking letters, wrapped in a faded red ribbon.

He slid the top letter out and opened it.

Dear Belle,

Well Christ almighty, it sure *seems* like you must have planned it. Don't get so flustered, sister, you're not the only one in the soup.

I'm enclosing a check, a big one. Do what you think is right with it.

I guess I'll see you when you get back out here to the Coast.

The scrawl at the bottom of the page was his father's signature.

More interesting was the date at the top: just six months before R.J. was born.

He opened the next letter. Again, it was from his father to his mother.

Glad you like your new apartment, although that's not what I thought you'd do with the check.

Some of the boys upstairs at the studio are very worried about you having this kid. They say it will kill your career, and do a lot of damage to mine. You don't want that, any more than I do, kiddo.

So the story they've come up with, after a long sitdown with your agent and my agent, is that we got married secretly last year while we were shooting *Double Negative*. Then we can secretly get married for *real* as soon as you can get your smooth pink rear end out here to Hollywood.

I know it's not exactly moonlight and roses, Belle, and I'm sure not going down on one knee, but the PR guys think this could be a terrific boost for both of us, and I'm all for that.

How about it, kid?

R.J. felt like he was rooted to the chair with a grand piano on his lap. He couldn't stand up to save his life.

There couldn't be any doubt about it: His parents had gotten married as a PR move because his mother was already pregnant. With him.

So much for the storybook romance crap he'd heard all his life. So much for the old issue of *LIFE* he still had, with the cover photo of the two of them, looking so lovey-dovey. Just another posed shot. Another scene played out like the studio wanted it.

What was that like? An arranged marriage—

arranged, not by parents who "only want the best," but by a bunch of pot-bellied, cigar-smoking weasels with too many consonants in their names.

They had married because of him. Jesus, had they even *liked* each other? Attracted to each other, sure. The rough, macho leading man, idol of millions; and the long-stemmed American beauty on her way to the top. Instant sack time.

But had they liked each other? Cared about each other? Held hands when they were alone, or only for the cameras? Had they done everything just for the cameras and lived totally separate lives on their own? Had their whole life together just been an elaborate movie set?

When it came down to that, then who the hell was he?

His head was spinning. Christ, he'd come here looking for answers, and all he had was a whole truckload of new questions.

He sat there for a long time, holding the letters in his hand.

It was getting dark outside when R.J. snapped out of it. He was left with the realization that he had never really known his mother.

He was long used to not knowing his father, who had died too long ago, when R.J. was just a kid. They hadn't had much time together, what with the old man's busy work schedule and all.

Sometimes R.J. thought he knew the old man better from his movies than from real life. But he was comfortable with that. It was just one of those things. Lots of people never knew their dads, especially in Hollywood.

But now his mother was gone too. She'd been there,

all the years of his life, and now she was dead and he didn't really know who she had been.

And that meant he didn't really know who *he* was either.

He ran a hand through his hair, rubbed his eyes. Get a grip, R.J., he told himself. All he had to do was throw some crap in a box, call Goodwill, and get out of here. He didn't need to take a swan dive off the deep end of his soul. Not now. He had a murderer to catch.

He put the letters back in the drawer.

The next drawer held a flowered book. It was one of those blank-paged books they sell at stationery stores. He flipped it open.

The book was about half filled with his mother's neat, spidery handwriting. It was a diary.

At least he could page through it, see if there was anything in it that might give him a hint about her killer. He started reading at a date three weeks back, when his mother had arrived in New York.

He was surprised at how well she wrote. Not that she'd ever been ditzy or anything, but the entries showed a clear-thinking woman who knew who she was and what she wanted—and, more often than not, how to get it.

There were some savagely funny drawings on the facing pages, pictures of people she knew, things she had seen that day. They were accompanied by very sharp comments.

If only he'd known. This was a hell of a bright, funny lady.

He found nothing in the diary that gave him even a faint clue to her death. She mentioned that she had a new boyfriend, Robert. That was the guy she was killed with. An analysis of his character that was only slightly flattering. Mentioned that he was miffed about going to a hell of a lot of trouble to exchange some hard-to-get tickets because she wouldn't go—it conflicted with her AA meeting.

R.J. put the book back where he found it.

He tilted back in the chair, his fingers locked behind his neck. He wished he'd known this side of his mother. So often people get locked into parts and have to play-act them, no matter what. Mother. Son. Boss, lover, babysitter. Can't break out and be yourself because you're already somebody else as far as the other person is concerned.

Play-acting. Like the killer. Deadly play-acting.

A funny thought hit him and he sat up straight. The diary he had seen only went back about six months. But it was so easy, so well done, he couldn't believe she had just started writing in a diary six months ago.

There had to be more diaries, maybe dating all the way back to when he was a kid. Maybe even beyond.

He got out of the chair and started looking around the room.

He finally found them at the back of the closet. There was a small bookshelf shoved all the way back, behind some old fur coats on hangers. There were about forty volumes, each with a small label on the spine telling the dates.

Don't be a snoop, he thought. Leave her some privacy. But this was all he had of her now, all he would ever have, and he wanted to know her better. He took down a volume from when he was about eleven and went back to the chair.

That year started to come back to him. It had been a hard year for R.J., but there were harder ones yet to come.

"The kid had that dream again last night," he read on a page as he flipped through. He stopped turning pages and read the entry.

He'd been having it almost every night back
around the time of the accident, but I thought we
were past all that now. I guess not.

He says The Scary Guy is trying to get him
again. He's very sure about that "again" part. He
says it's The Scary Guy that wrecked his bike,
come back to kill him. . . .

The accident. It all came back to him. The year
before, when he was ten, some maniac in a car had run
over him, crushed his bike, broken his wrist, and left
him with the funny scar in the dimple on his chin.

R.J. was so positive about seeing The Scary Guy
all over, everywhere we went, for a couple of
weeks before the accident. It's funny how his little
mind works. I'm sure it was just some drunk who
got scared and took off when he saw he'd hit a
kid. But R.J. is convinced it's some kind of plot,
that the guy had been following him for two
weeks first.

But he *hadn't* been following R.J.—he'd been following Belle! And damn it, he was *still* sure about that.

He'd seen that same face, everywhere they went together, for two weeks. His mother had been cast in a
picture at the time, but it hadn't started shooting. They
were still casting the other parts, so she'd had some
time. Even taken him to the park once.

And The Scary Guy had been *there* too! All dressed
up as an ice-cream vendor, wearing a big fake mustache, but it had been him, no doubt about it.

Just a stalker, probably. A celebrity stalker. They
didn't have a name for it back then. Now they were all
over the place. Even the local TV weatherman had
one.

R.J. hadn't thought about The Scary Guy for years. But he remembered him now. He remembered the dreams too.

In the dreams The Scary Guy would be coming at him from everywhere. Every face he saw, even faces he knew like Mom and his teachers, would suddenly melt into the blank, ordinary face of The Scary Guy. And somehow that everyday face was more frightening than all the bogeymen he had ever dreamed up before. Something in the eyes, maybe, like they were bland gray caves where an animal was crouching, ready to spring out at him.

The Scary Guy. Geez. R.J. shook his head. Then he read some more.

CHAPTER 13

In the middle of the night he sat straight up in his mother's bed covered with sweat. He could still hear the echo of his own gasping.

He'd had the dream again, the one he used to have when he was a kid. The Scary Guy was back, trying to kill him. Only this time his face swam into focus in more recent form. He was the drunk and the priest, the people R.J. had been looking at on Casey's tapes.

R.J. turned on the bedside light and swung his feet onto the floor. He rubbed his face, hoping to get some blood flowing. What a schmuck, scared out of his wits by a dream he used to have when he was ten. Seeing that face again, in the drunk, the priest, the newsman. He was letting the strain get to him.

He stood up and walked toward the bathroom and stopped cold halfway there.

What newsman?

He played the dream back in his head. It was already

fading, the way dreams do once you're awake and out of bed. R.J. grabbed hard at the wisps of it that were left.

At the funeral, the priest turned away from the grave and looked at him, and it was The Scary Guy. He ran. Nightmare running, where you don't go anywhere. Tombstones moving past with terrible, deadly slowness. A man leaning on one of them. He runs to the man for help—it's The Scary Guy again. He turns around to run—and there's The Scary Guy, swinging a microphone at him like a broadsword. About to lop his head off.

And R.J. woke up, yelling.

Where had he seen that reporter? Was he making it up, creating a figure out of his anger and frustration with the jackals that had been on him all day at the funeral?

No. He'd seen the guy, actually seen him. Where?

The funeral home.

It came to him in a bright flash of memory. Stepping out of the funeral home toward the limo. The crowd surging at him. One reporter in particular shoving brutally forward, ramming the microphone into his face. Something wrong with the face, something not reporterlike—what?

The eyes.

That was it. The eyes, those same terrible gray eyes, like some evil, diseased animal's eyes, in that bland, ordinary face. He hadn't noticed it consciously, but his subconscious had taken note and brought it back up in the dream.

It was him.

It was The Scary Guy.

The Scary Guy had killed his mother.

He tried to laugh it off, make it into the funny quirk of an overworked, emotionally exhausted brain trying to turn tragedy into something that made sense.

Tried like hell. Couldn't do it.

The Scary Guy had killed his mother.

━━━━━━━━━━━━━━━◆━━━━━━━━━━━━━━━

"Jesus Christ, R.J.," Casey Wingate said, "do you have any idea what time it is?"

"I've got to see the tapes," R.J. said. "I don't give a rat's ass what time it is. I've got to see them now."

He could hear her blow a heavy stream of air through pursed lips. "Come on over," she said and hung up.

It was easier to flag a taxi from the swank neighborhood of Central Park West than it had ever been from his own apartment. In half an hour from the time he called he was down at Casey's in the Village.

He was so hot to see the tapes that he barely noticed how good Casey looked in the old terrycloth bathrobe she'd thrown on. Holding the robe closed with one hand, she led him over to her ministudio and turned on the first tape.

"What is all this, R.J.?" she asked. "Why does it have to be now? At three-thirty in the morning, for God's sake?"

"I think I remembered where I know the guy from," he said, staring at the screen. "I have to check—stop!"

Once again he looked at the drunk, at the haunting familiarity of his fleshy face. Mentally, R.J. stripped away the jowls, the red, bulbous nose. It could be. It could be him.

"Next tape."

She slammed in number two and wound it forward with the joystick.

"Stop."

And there was the priest. Again he tried to be sure, and he couldn't, but he was almost sure. Almost.

"What do you have from today?"

Casey blinked, still not fully awake.

"Footage," he told her impatiently. "From today."

"Today?" she said. "What would you like?"

"The mob scene, coming out of the funeral home. Did you get any of that?"

"I was right behind you," she said.

"Let's see it," he said.

She moved over to the counter and went through a stack of six or seven tapes in hard black plastic covers, checking numbers on the sides. "Got it," she said, opening one of the cases and pushing it into a three-quarter deck.

The tape started with background shots of the funeral home, the crowd outside, the mob scene in the street. It moved inside past the coffin and around the room before cutting to R.J. coming in the door, flanked by Hookshot and Portillo.

The tape went on to the service without a break, and Casey ran it forward at its fastest speed. The tape hit the end, and she rewound it a bit.

"Let's try here," she said, putting it up on screen again.

R.J. was walking toward the outside door, and then he was outside. The crowd surged up at him; Portillo and Hookshot helped him push toward the—

"Stop! Right there, back it up a little. Now freeze."

The tape jerked to a halt and R.J. leaned forward, not even breathing.

It was him. The microphone held out, the blazer with the patch just barely visible: CABLE INDEPENDENT NEWS.

Same face, no doubt about that. Disguised a little, subtly changed—the guy was very good at that, *very* fucking good. It was the same guy as the drunk, the priest, he was almost positive.

Almost.

But even that wasn't as hard to believe as the other. How could it possibly be the face out of his boyhood nightmares? It was not even remotely conceivable that that same face was back, that it had killed his mother and now wanted to kill him. It just wasn't possible.

Was it?

"What is it?"

He almost jerked up out of his seat at Casey's question. He'd forgotten where he was, forgotten she was there. And that's a very bad sign, he thought, to forget legs like those.

"What is it, R.J.?" she repeated.

"I'm not sure," he said, "but I think I know the guy."

"Who is he?" she rasped, leaning forward, her eyes burning. As she leaned forward she showed a little more cleavage than she might have liked.

"Uh—" He stopped cold, took a deep breath. "I think—he's the guy that gave me this," he said, fingering the scar on his chin.

She didn't say anything for a minute, which he thought was pretty decent of her, considering what he was asking her to believe. "Go on," she said finally, sitting back again.

He told her the whole thing, the whole story of The Scary Guy, how it had come back to him reading the diaries, and how he couldn't shake the idea now that this was the same guy, come out of the past, out of his nightmares, to kill his mother.

When he was done, she didn't say anything for a long time.

"You think I'm nuts," he said.

She tossed her hair back. "I don't know you well enough to think that," she said. "But even if you're right, I don't see what good it does you. You didn't know who the guy was then, and you still don't."

"Yeah, I know. But it's more than I knew before. Maybe the cops have something that can help."

Casey snorted. "If they do, they probably don't know they have it. But I'll tell you one thing interesting," she said, recrossing her legs.

"What's that?" asked R.J., trying hard not to look.

She flashed a smile. "There's no such thing as Cable Independent News."

CHAPTER 14

It was only a little after seven o'clock in the morning when R.J. climbed the steps into NYPD headquarters. No way he could sleep, and he was gambling that Angelo Bertelli was the kind of cop who came early and stayed late. R.J. was sure that in spite of the flashy suit and the easy smile, Bertelli was a hard-working cop.

But Bertelli wasn't in yet, according to the tough-looking woman in the sergeant's uniform who was sitting behind the front desk. So R.J. went out to the newspaper box just outside the station and grabbed a paper. He sat down on a hard chair inside and started to read.

The goddamn Mets. They couldn't beat a Little League team. And a couple of them probably ought to be in jail. What the hell was the game coming to?

"This is a pleasant surprise," sneered an unpleasant voice, and R.J. looked up to see Kates giving him a cold glare.

"Lieutenant," said R.J. affably. "What brings you down here? Didn't think there were any butts around to kiss at this hour."

Kates flushed bright red. "Listen, Mr. Fontaine—or whatever you're calling yourself nowadays—you're gonna need a favor before too long, and when you do—"

"Don't come crawling to you, Freddy?" R.J. finished for him. "Thanks for the tip. I'll see if I can stay alive without you." And he flipped the newspaper back open again.

Out of the corner of his eye, R.J. could see Kates clenching and unclenching his hands for a good thirty seconds before he finally stomped away.

R.J. was a bit guilty about how good it made him feel to get to Kates like that. Too easy, he thought, I need a challenge. But he was also aware that the lieutenant would be a dangerous enemy if he got the chance. And he was pretty sure that Kates was right: He was going to need a friend before this was over.

I shouldn't rag him like that, he thought. But what the hell. A guy has to have a hobby.

He was finished with the sports and working on the crossword puzzle when Bertelli came in ten minutes later. "Hey, Angelo," R.J. called, and the young cop came over and stuck out his hand.

"How ya doin', R.J.?" he said.

"I need a favor," R.J. replied.

Bertelli blinked. "Geez, you're supposed to beat around the bush for a minute or two, shoot the breeze, you know."

"Sorry, I was up all night." As he said it, R.J. realized how tired he was. He shook the feeling off. There was no time for being tired now. When this was over he could sleep a week.

"What've you got?" Bertelli asked him. His eyes were shining with eagerness.

R.J. frowned. "I'm not sure," he said. "I might have something—but it's not much. I need to look at your case file, see if you got anything that backs it up."

Bertelli looked thoughtful. "That's a big favor," he said slowly. "The Looie would chew my ass right off for that. I've talked too much already. No, I'm sorry, R.J., I don't see how I can do that." He shook his head sorrowfully. "Unless you can trade me something."

R.J. smiled, just a little. "You're a sly bastard, aren't you, Angelo?"

Bertelli spread his hands, palms up. "Hey, that's life, R.J. What're you gonna do?" And now he grinned. "So how's about it? Got a trade for me?"

R.J. shrugged and spread his hands. "I'd like to, but it's not up to me. You got a few minutes?"

"Whattaya got in mind?"

"Maybe we could meet somebody for a cup of coffee."

"Somebody who could make the trade?"

R.J. nodded. "That's right. How about it?"

Bertelli hesitated for a moment, then shrugged. "Lemme check my desk first. Be right back." He clapped R.J. on the shoulder and, nodding to the paper, said, "Twenty-seven across is *sabots.*" He turned and walked quickly to the stairs.

R.J. glanced down at the crossword puzzle. Bertelli was right.

———————————◆———————————

Casey had agreed to meet them for coffee at a joint a couple of blocks away, but she'd been dubious about it, especially about meeting with a cop. "Angelo is different," R.J. had said.

And now he was wishing that Bertelli *wasn't* so different. It was clear that he was charming the hell out of Casey Wingate.

A simple cup of coffee turned into croissants and cappuccino, and Bertelli was in charge all the way. He was "Angelo" now to Casey, had been "Angelo" almost at once.

Casey said, "How do you, Officer Bertelli?" and he flinched away like she'd slapped him.

"Oh, *gesu*, please, don't call me that, you're breaking my heart." He placed a hand over his heart and looked like he would faint.

"All right then, what do I call you?"

He snapped almost to attention, took her hand and kissed it, like some goddamned count out of one of Belle's old movies. "Call me 'Angelo,' " he said. "It's my name."

And Casey *giggled*! The sound was shocking to R.J., a girlish giggle coming out of hard-boiled Casey. He couldn't believe it.

Worse than that, he realized he was clenching his fists and sizing up Bertelli as if they were about to slug it out.

But I like this guy. Am I jealous? R.J. asked himself. Of what? There's nothing to be jealous about.

Is there?

As he thought it, Casey laughed, throwing her head back to reveal a sleek neck.

Hell yes, plenty, he thought, tuning back in on their banter.

"I don't want to interrupt," he said, and two pairs of cool, amused eyes turned to him. "But can we get this deal done?"

"No problem, R.J.," said Bertelli. "How's about it, Miss Wingate?"

She smiled at him. Damn that Italian charm, R.J. thought.

"It's really not up to me. But—R.J., why don't you bring Angelo up to date first?"

R.J. nodded. He told the whole thing: the dreams, the childhood accident, the man on the tapes. He tried to make it sound as objective and hard-edged as possible, but it was tough sledding.

Bertelli didn't interrupt. He just sat with one finger to his chin, every now and then glancing at Casey and raising an eyebrow.

When R.J. was done, Bertelli shrugged. "It ain't a lot," he said. "But it's a lot more than I got right now. Okay, I'll show you the file. When can I see the tapes?"

Casey hesitated, then said, "Angelo, I'm sorry if I misled you. I can't let you see the tapes—*officially.*"

"What does that mean?"

"You, personally, can come see them right now if you want. But I can't release them into evidence—they're not my property."

Bertelli shook his head. "If you'd leave the table for just a moment, Miss Wingate, I'd like to say a very bad word."

"Look," R.J. butted in, "the problem before was that this asshole Pike wanted to make you get a warrant, and it's too much trouble if you don't even know the tapes are worth it. So now you know: They're worth it. Get the warrant."

"How sure are you that this guy on the tapes is the killer?" asked Bertelli.

R.J. raised an eyebrow. "What else have you got?"

"Besides," Casey added, with a touch of humor R.J. hadn't seen before, "anything that gets Pike's nuts in a knot is worth doing."

"Ouch," said Bertelli, "this woman plays hardball."

"Finish your coffee," said R.J. "Let's go."

But after two hours with the police files, R.J. was

ready to admit that the cop had gotten the better of the swap.

Bertelli had put them in an out-of-the-way interrogation room and sat them down. He'd carried a cardboard box in, thumped it down on the table with a hearty "Here it is," and left them to go through it.

When they had finished, the only thing they knew that they hadn't before was that neither of the victims had any trace of alcohol or drugs in their bodies at the time of death. Since Belle had been sober for a number of years, that wasn't exactly a major break in the case.

"I'm late," said Casey, abruptly slamming shut the last folder and tossing it back in the box. "And this is getting us nowhere."

R.J. stood up and stretched. "I'll walk you out." He had finished first and had just been watching her read.

They walked down to Bertelli's cubbyhole. R.J. stuck his head in. "All done," he said. "Thanks for nothing."

"Back at you, buddy," the detective said.

R.J. started toward the exit, where Casey was waiting, but a shout from Bertelli brought him to a stop.

"Hey, R.J.!"

Bertelli walked three steps toward R.J.

"You let me know, huh? If you find something?"

"You do the same, Angelo," he said.

As R.J. walked out onto the sidewalk with Casey, he heard a minor tussle off to his left, punctuated by a squalling sound. He turned to look.

Coming toward him was a pert, overly made-up blonde in a blazer, holding a microphone and trailed by a cameraman.

"Mr. Brooks!" she said excitedly, and R.J. recognized the squalling sound he'd just heard.

"No comment," R.J. said and turned away.

"But I'm from 'Entertainment Tonight'!" she fog-horned at him.

"In that case," said R.J., "I have a comment—but you can't use it on the air."

"Don't you want to tell your side of the story? We'll let you do that."

"Lay off him, you hussy," Casey said, taking R.J. by the elbow. "He's with me."

And, stifling a giggle, she led him away from the out-raged ET reporter. "The hell with you, Wingate!" the blonde called after.

"Thanks," R.J. told her.

"Thanks nothing," she retorted. "You promised me an exclusive, and you're going to stick to that promise."

"You bet I will," he said. "You're the only media slug I ever want to talk to."

"Of course. Because you know I'll get your story right."

"Sure," he said. "You can think that, if you want to."

A drink is really all he needs.

There.

Much better now. Absolutely no cause for concern, not of any kind. The son is on the hook, and he will be drawn in, gaffed and netted. It's really quite simple, quite certain.

Smooth down the small wrinkle on the sleeve of his uniform coat. The gold braid on the sleeve catches the dim light in the bar, and the sight pleases him.

On the stool beside him is the hat of a lieutenant commander in the Argentinian navy. He strokes his pencil-thin mustache with one thumb and reaches for his drink.

Ah. It is very good. The drink—and the son; watching him flail about, squirm, thinking he is the hunter, when in fact he is the prey. Oh, yes, it was a rich irony, one he loved deeply. All great theater has a certain amount of irony, and this—

Well. This was going to be his masterpiece. It was too complex for the stage, just as he himself was too complex. The fools never could see beyond his face—couldn't see that the face they said was too bland was actually his greatest tool! The thing that made him great!

Idiots!

The greatest talent of his time, beyond any question, and they couldn't see it, wouldn't see it, wouldn't look beyond the envelope to the raging fire inside, the brilliant talent that could sit astride the stage like a colossus. Why? Because he was too plain-looking?! Because he seemed ordinary?! Because—

But enough.

He signals for another drink.

He will show them. He will make it so clear that even those idiots couldn't miss it. They could keep their films, their Broadway roles, and he would be content with regional dinner theater. Because he has at last found the way to express himself. Great talent must out, and his was. In his own pure art form, so far beyond their simple little skits.

Even the stupidest of them could not fail to see. When you actually see the talent in its full bloom, ah, how different it is then.

He is starting to feel that small tickle, all the way at the back of his mind, the little, almost imperceptible twinge that says it is time to do something again.

Still time to set the scene properly, yes, plenty of time for that, but . . .

Perhaps he should pick up the pace a little. Try something odd, different. An attack from an oblique angle.

Yes. He sips his drink. Something unexpected, that will be interesting.

Then they would see.

CHAPTER 15

The man was a prick, there was no doubt about it and no other word for it. He was a fat, pale, pumpkin-assed, dickless little prick.

Casey hadn't said so, not in so many words, because Pike was well connected and turning a good dollar for his board of directors. But she had let him know what she thought. It didn't seem to bother him much.

Somehow he'd figured out it was her fault the cops had showed up with a warrant. And he threw an absolute tiff.

"Wingate!" His voice warbled down the hall. And Pike came waddling after it, his arms and legs pumping in a furious cartoon of roly-poly rage.

And he poured himself into her office, his fat little finger coming up into her face and shaking like an enraged cocktail weenie.

She almost laughed at the sight of this pudgy, bug-eyed little asshole, stomping his feet and screaming in a shrill and trembling voice.

And why? The tapes were not a big deal—except that *he* had said the cops couldn't see them, and his lawyers had said he had to let them.

Prick.

Casey grabbed up her handbag and headed for the elevator, leaving the little lardball in midtirade.

Anyway, the cops would get the tapes—or copies of them, to be accurate. Maybe they'd even send Angelo to pick them up—whoops, Detective Bertelli. She'd have to be careful about that around the office.

The elevator doors slid open. She stepped in and punched the button for the lobby.

Still, he was a sweet guy, for a cop. Something about the eyes, she thought. Or—no, he just had It. Whatever It was.

Some very unlikely looking people had It: Pavarotti, Woody Allen, and Bertelli. Funny. None of them good-looking guys, not like R.J. . . .

Now where had that thought come from?

The elevator stopped. Casey strode out, nodding to the guard.

"Going home early, Miss Wingate?"

"That's right, Bobby."

"Well, good night then." The beefy old man smiled at her. She knew he was watching her legs as she stepped out onto the street, but what the hell, let him dream.

R.J. Brooks, handsome? This was the first time the thought had come to her consciously. She looked at it for a minute as she scanned for a taxi.

He wasn't actually *bad*-looking. A little battered, maybe, but that had its charm. The chin was good, very firm, and the scar was intriguing, especially now that she knew how he'd gotten it. And of course, those fantastic eyes, so very much like his mother's.

She saw a cab cruising and stepped to the curb, raising her hand.

He certainly didn't have any fat on him. Not like that little prick Pike. Still, R.J. handsome? Why was she thinking about this anyway? Maybe she was—

She became aware that the cab was heading straight at her.

And it was not slowing down.

Casey blinked. Surely it would squeal to a stop. It was just racing to get to her quickly, looking for a bigger tip, trying to beat out a rival, that was all. It would brake—it would brake right now.

It didn't brake. It sped up.

R.J. leaned back in his office chair, thinking. He thought of what he knew about the creep that killed his mother, which was almost nothing.

He thought about what he could do to find out more, which seemed about the same.

He ground his teeth. The frustration made him want a drink. Sure, he thought, that'll help a lot. Get drunk. Cry in your beer.

He pushed the thought of a drink away and realized he was hungry. He was just thinking about asking Wanda to go get him a sandwich, when he heard the outer door slam open, and a few seconds later Casey Wingate stormed in.

She was a mess, but the most gorgeous mess he'd ever seen. Her hair was everywhere, her clothes were dirty and even torn in a couple of places. Her stockings were shredded. She looked great.

But her eyes were spouting flames, and the color in her face didn't need any makeup at all.

She came into the office like a bolt of long-legged lightning and Wanda was right behind her. R.J. waved her off.

"It's okay, Wanda. This is Casey Wingate."

Wanda gave Casey the kind of once-over only another woman can manage and nodded. She slid out and pulled the door closed.

"Well, Miss Wingate—" he started to say. He didn't get very far with it. Casey put both knuckles on his desk and leaned in at him, looking like an avenging angel.

"He tried to kill me, R.J.," she said.

R.J. sat up straight. "Who did?"

"The killer, the man who killed your mother. He just tried for me, not fifteen minutes ago!"

"Did you see him? Are you sure it was him?"

"Who the hell else wants to kill me?"

R.J. let that one go. "All right, what happened?"

"I'm in front of my office, flagging down a cab, and the son of a bitch comes straight at me!"

"Casey, cab drivers in this city—"

She stopped him. "I've lived here all my life, I know all about Manhattan cab drivers. This guy came right up on the sidewalk after me. After *me*, R.J.—not anybody else on the sidewalk."

"How did he miss you?"

She glared at him. "You sound disappointed. Look at this!"

She hiked up her skirt and showed him her ruined stockings. "I had to dive behind a telephone pole. The bastard smacked the pole and drove off, smirking at me."

"You saw him smirk? What does he look like?"

"Dark-skinned, bearded, with thick black horn-rimmed glasses. He looked like all the ten thousand Pakistani cab drivers in the city."

"Except—"

"What?" He was impressed with how cool she was, how many details she had noticed. This was a very tough woman, he thought. Tough and drop-dead gorgeous—an incredible combination.

She shrugged. "It was only a quick glance, and I was lying on the pavement, madder than hell. So I could be wrong. But it sure *looked* like he had gray eyes."

He had managed to get a chair under her as she talked it through, right up to the part about the driver's eyes. Now he stood up straight and had to concentrate on breathing.

"How sure are you?" R.J. asked her.

She shook her head. "Maybe ninety percent. He looked right at me, almost like he was mocking me. Like he wanted me to—" She broke off and frowned.

"Like he wanted you to know he could have got you if he'd wanted to?"

"Well—yes."

R.J. nodded. "That's what I'm thinking too. It doesn't fit the way he likes to kill. So if he missed you—"

"Then maybe he *wanted* to miss me," she finished. "But why?"

R.J. stood up. "If he's sending a message, I'm not getting it. So it's more likely he's just playing with me."

Casey looked outraged. "With *you*?! Jesus Christ, R.J., he nearly squashed me, and he's playing with *you*?"

He shrugged. "Sorry. But that's what I think. I think he's after me, and he's just poking around at the people that he knows I care about—"

He stopped, aware he'd said something without thinking, something he hadn't meant to say. But Casey didn't appear to notice.

"All right, I see what you're saying. But if he kills me

I'll still be dead, R.J., even if he's killing me just to piss you off."

"You got a point," R.J. conceded. "And he might try again." A thought occurred to him. If this guy knew where Casey worked . . . "I think I'll take you home," he said.

Casey stared at him with disgust. "I'm a big girl, R.J." she said. "I'm not going to wilt and get all weepy. I'll be fine." She stood up.

"I'm sure you will be," he said. "But if he's waiting for you at your apartment, this could be my best shot at catching him. I'm coming with you."

"Oh. I see what you mean. Uh, actually, I'd love some company."

They caught a cab down to the Village, dodging Wanda's dirty look on the way out. The midday traffic was as bad as ever, and the trip took almost half an hour.

They got out in front of Casey's building, and R.J. took her arm and led her to the front door. She unlocked it and started in, but R.J. gently pushed her back. She raised an eyebrow as he stepped in the door ahead of her.

"We have to assume he was watching the street," he said. "So he knows we're here now."

"If *he's* here."

He gave her a quick hard smile. "Let's assume the worst," he said, reaching back to the hollow of his spine. He pulled his gun, feeling just a little better already, just to have that solid, reassuring weight in his hand.

"What *is* that thing?" she asked, slightly amused in spite of the tension.

"That's the Big E," he told her. "Stay behind us."

She obediently stepped behind him, but not without

muttering under her breath, "R.J. Rambo."

Going up the stairs he hugged the wall, using extra caution at the landing. A staircase can hold some nasty surprises. He knew that, not just from his work, but from the tony private boarding schools his mother had stuck him in.

Kids in places like that had no mercy. No mercy at all, but plenty of imagination, and generally enough money to make their mean little dreams come true.

But this was no kid's prank. This was a killer, and the things his school chums had done, as bad as they had been, weren't even in the same league.

Arriving at the door to Casey's floor, he motioned her to stay put and went up one more flight. Nothing. He went back down.

Again signaling without sound, he waved her several feet back, away from any possible line of fire from the door.

Crouching low, he swung the door open and rolled through, gun ready.

Nothing; the empty hallway sneered at him.

The carpet was old and dirty too. R.J. found he was lying in a spot of some kind of grease. It smelled like somebody had cooked a wet dog and poured out the grease afterward.

Casey stuck her head around the corner. "Hey, James Bond, is it safe to come out?"

R.J. stood up and brushed himself off. "It's safe," he said. "Stay close to the wall."

He kept her about ten feet behind him as he inched along the wall, trying to look everywhere, anticipate every possibility.

If it was me, I'd get in the doorway right across, he thought. And he kept his gun in that direction.

But then he thought, But it's not me. This guy is a loon. He could be anywhere.

He paused a few feet away from Casey's door.

Something looked wrong. He couldn't put his finger on what, but something was just a little off.

The downstairs door thumped as somebody came in or went out. A slight breeze moved down the hall.

Casey's door trembled and then opened slightly.

R.J. felt his heart thundering. *The killer had been here.*

He waved furiously at Casey to move back. She cocked her head as though she didn't quite get it. He waved harder, and she shrugged and moved back.

Crouching again, R.J. duck-walked slowly and quietly toward the door. Reaching out his left hand, he pushed the door open all the way.

The place was trashed.

The couch had been flipped onto its back and slashed open. The canvas chairs were shredded. Piles of Casey's clothes were flung in the center of the room. All the food and drink from the refrigerator had been poured over them.

"R.J.? What is it?"

"Get back!" he hissed at her. He straightened and flattened himself to one side of the doorway. He looked up and down the hall quickly.

"I'm going in," he said softly. "If you hear anything at all—*anything*—just pull the fire alarm." He pointed his gun at the alarm on the wall beside her. "That'll get them here fast and make a lot of commotion too."

He could see her take a breath, then whisper to him, "Good luck." Then he was through the door.

R.J. was reasonably sure the killer was gone already. But he knew plenty of guys who'd wound up with a tag on their toe from a sure thing.

So he moved slowly and carefully through the rooms, trying to keep his gun barrel moving from one possible point of danger to the next.

The closet.

Window curtains.

Under the bed.

The shower.

Nothing.

The guy was gone. But he'd done a very thorough job before he left.

There was not one piece of furniture, article of clothing, or item of food that he had not touched, ripped, slashed, soaked, flung, stained. He was a meticulous maniac, thought R.J.

When he was certain the place was empty, he stepped back into the hall.

Casey was watching the doorway with fierce concentration, one hand on the fire alarm.

"It ain't pretty," R.J. told her, "but it's okay to come in now."

She came inside, turning to look with amazement at her totaled apartment. "Holy shit," she said. "Holy fucking shit." She bent and picked up her bathrobe, shook it. A small shower of rice and a glob of yogurt fell off onto the floor.

"Everything," she said. "Every fucking thing I own. Oh well." She turned a tattered chair over and sank into it. "It's only stuff."

R.J. was more astonished by her reaction than by anything else he'd seen in a long time. "That's it?" he said. "You're not going to start screaming and kicking things? Jesus, Casey," he said, shaking his head, "you really are something. If it was me, I'd be yelling and breaking anything that isn't broken. I thought you'd have a shit-fit."

She shrugged. "R.J., it's just stuff. *Things.* Some of them are nice, but it's not that important. What matters to me is my work, and nobody—Oh my God!" She lurched up off the couch to her ministudio.

"Shit," she said, "shit shit *SHIT*."

"What? For Christ's sake, what?"

She turned to R.J. "They're gone. The tapes are gone."

CHAPTER 16

Sorry, Brooks," said Lieutenant Kates, but he didn't sound sorry; it's hard to sound sorry with a sneer on your face. "I don't see anything that connects it. It has all the earmarks of a standard B&E. That's what my report will call it."

They stood in the ruins of Casey's apartment. The lab crew had been over everything with magnifying glasses, dusted every possible surface for prints, run dozens of small tests. Like Kates said, they'd found nothing.

"There's no fingerprints on this either," said a voice behind R.J.

He turned to see Boggs with a smirk on his face and a pair of Casey's panties held up on the end of a pencil. "No fingerprints at all. You slowing down, Brooks? Losing your touch?"

R.J. stepped right into Boggs's face, putting his foot

down hard on the cop's toes. Boggs grunted with pain.

"If you'll leave your badge with the lieutenant for a minute," R.J. said, an inch from his nose, "there's a few things I'd like to show you out in the hall."

"Knock it off, Brooks!" said Kates. "Boggs, try hard not to be an asshole. Just for five minutes, okay?"

Boggs didn't look at Kates. "Any time, any place, Brooks," he said under his breath.

"I'll be right there waiting," R.J. told him and stepped away.

R.J. turned to Kates. "That's it, huh? That's your theory? This was an unconnected break-in, just your garden-variety B&E?"

"That's what goes in my report," the lieutenant said.

"But that's not what you think," R.J. said.

"No, it's not."

"You want to share that one with me? I could use a laugh."

Now it was Kates who moved close, getting up into R.J.'s face. "I'd love to share it with you, smart-ass. And we'll see if you can laugh it off.

"I think you and the bimbo did this yourself."

R.J. blinked. "Are you serious?"

"Very serious, Brooks. Go ahead and laugh. I think you did it so you wouldn't have to hand over the tapes. And I think you and that broad are up to something funny, and this is all aimed at getting publicity."

"Come off it, Kates."

"Brooks, everybody knows you've had your problems with booze, and probably drugs. And then you toss in that high-class bloodline you got. Guys like you get hungry for the spotlight. Especially when you start hitting the bottle again. How come you're not laughing now, Brooks?"

R.J. shook his head. "Freddy, I always knew you

were meaner than a snake, but I never took you for stupid. But if you seriously believe that, I'm going to have to rethink some things."

"Start by rethinking what you'll do for a living when I yank your license for conspiracy to withhold evidence," said Kates, turning away.

R.J. watched him go. I should have seen it coming, he thought. Kates's been looking for an excuse to nail my ass for years. If I don't give him a reason, he'll invent one—and he thinks this is it.

He ground his teeth. Let him think what he wants. I'm not getting sidetracked, or scared off, or stopped. Not this time.

R.J. went out into the hall. Casey was there, getting a thorough grilling from Angelo Bertelli. At least R.J. assumed it was a grilling. Something about the way Bertelli placed a hand on her shoulder, the flash of his teeth as he asked her questions, made him think Bertelli was doing a little more than conducting an investigation.

But even worse was the way Casey smiled back at him, touched his hand as she answered; the way she stood just slightly too close to him for someone being questioned by a cop.

And why should that matter? R.J. wondered. It's a free country, and I don't have any claim on her. But he still ground his teeth.

Bertelli looked up when he saw R.J. and beckoned him over with a twist of his head.

"Sorry about all this, R.J.," Bertelli said, folding his notebook closed and stuffing it into the inside pocket of his elegant charcoal-gray suit.

"Don't tell me, tell Miss Wingate," R.J. said.

"I did. And I mean it. To both of you."

"Do you think the two of us did this ourselves, for publicity?" R.J. asked him.

Casey gasped in outrage. "Did Kates say that?"

"He did," R.J. told her.

"And you think that too, Angelo?"

Bertelli shook his head. "No, I don't. That's mostly what I'm sorry about. But . . ." He gave a helpless shrug. "It don't much matter what I think. The lieutenant is the boss on this task force. So what he says goes."

"Which means this whole thing gets turned over to Robbery. Which means nothing happens."

Bertelli shrugged again. "That's about the size of it. Like I say, I'm sorry."

R.J. swore under his breath, but Casey patted Bertelli on the arm. "I know you mean well, Angelo. What is it you guys say? Fuggetaboudit."

He gave her a wink. "Thanks. You going to be all right? If you need a place to stay for a few days, 'til this gets cleaned up . . ."

R.J.'s blood boiled, but Casey was already shaking her head with a warm smile.

"I'll be fine, Angelo. Don't worry about me. I'll hole up in a hotel, hire a cleaning service."

"Okay," Bertelli said, looking at her long and hard. Then he turned to R.J. "Keep an eye on her, huh?"

"Sure, Angelo. That's easy. You got the hard job."

Bertelli cocked an eye at him. "What's that?"

R.J. nodded toward Kates and Boggs, huddled inside and talking in low voices. "Keeping those two clowns from shooting themselves in the ass. Let's get out of here, Casey."

He turned and started for the stairs. Casey came right behind him, pausing briefly to say goodbye to Bertelli. In a few moments they were out on the street.

"I'm hungry. How about a bite to eat?" he asked her.

She shrugged. "All right. Where to?"

He looked around. "Anyplace good around here?"

"There's a Mexican place a few blocks away."

R.J. shuddered. "No thanks. Mexican food in Manhattan is like French cooking in London. There isn't any, and you don't want to try the stuff they're saying is."

Casey snorted. "From what I knew about you, I didn't think you'd be so fussy."

"Well, I am about Mexican food. That's how I was brought up."

She looked at him curiously now. "Belle brought you up to be fussy about Mexican food?"

"Belle didn't bring me up at all."

"Then who—"

He took her arm again. "Come on. Let's get some food and I'll tell you all about it."

They found a place a few blocks away that was quiet and said they could do a pretty good omelet. It was in between a store selling leather pants and a jewelry shop that advertised a special on nipple-piercing. But the restaurant looked clean, and the smells coming from the kitchen were pretty good. Besides, R.J. was hungry enough to eat almost anything.

The waiter, a thin, middle-aged man with a neat mustache, flirted outrageously with R.J. But what the hell; it was the Village.

The omelet was pretty good; so was the coffee. R.J. had a ham, cheese, and onion omelet with hash browns, pumpernickel toast, and a pot of strawberry jam.

Casey ordered a cream cheese and caviar omelet. The sound of it made R.J. wince, but when it came it looked and smelled good, and he ended up finishing it when Casey had had enough.

While they ate, R.J. told Casey about his Uncle Hank and a lot more. She was a good listener, giving him all her attention and prompting with small questions, always at the right time. She seemed to want to know all about him, which was not all that surprising. After all, it was background for her story.

The surprise was that he wanted to tell her.

"So he's not really your uncle," Casey said when he had told her about Henry Portillo.

"More like my father," R.J. said.

She raised an eyebrow at him.

"I'm serious," he said. "A boy needs a man to teach him how he's supposed to behave. How to be a man—besides just shaving every morning, although that's important to learn right too. But with my father dead and my stepfather kind of temporary, I didn't have anybody to smack me when I did something stupid and tell me what I should have done. Until Uncle Hank."

"So he smacked you a lot?"

R.J. grinned. "Sure. I needed it a lot. But he took me to see the Dodgers too. Taught me how to use my fists and when it was right to use them. And more important, he taught me how to make *fajitas al carbon.*"

She was looking at him like she expected more, so he shrugged and said, "That's about it. Except whenever I really need a friend, Uncle Hank somehow knows about it and shows up."

"Your mother said he was a good family friend."

R.J. grinned. "He was that. And a lot more than that too. He was the kind of friend most people never have in Hollywood. He never gave a shit about how big a star somebody thought they were. All he cared about was what was right.

"I don't think Belle realized how much he did for us. But I'm glad she noticed that much."

They finished eating, had a last cup of coffee. R.J. felt he had talked a lot, more than he could remember talking to a woman before. This woman was getting to him, opening him up, making him feel things he hadn't felt in a while. He wasn't sure what he thought about that, but he knew he didn't want to go back.

The check came. R.J. reached for it automatically—but found Casey had darted a hand out and grabbed it first.

"Hey," he said. "What gives?"

"It's on me," she told him.

"Like hell it is. Give it here."

He held his hand out for the check. She smacked it away. "Knock it off," she said. "I said it's on me, and I mean it."

"But—"

"No buts," she said. She stuck a credit card on top of the check and handed it to the waiter, who gave her a half-bow, winked at R.J., and slithered away.

"What was all that?" he asked her.

"Is there a reason I shouldn't pick up the check?" she demanded.

"I was going to."

"Because you're the man, and you think you're supposed to."

"That's part of it," he said.

"What a load of horse shit," she said. "What did you make last year? Forty? Fifty?"

"None of your business," he said. But she was close—a little high, but close.

"I make a lot more than that, R.J. So why shouldn't I pay for dinner? I ate too, didn't I?"

"That isn't the point," he said.

"What is?" she demanded.

"When I take a woman to dinner, she shouldn't have to pay the check."

"She didn't *have* to. She just is."

"Well, I just was."

"Because of your masculine pride?" she asked.

"For God's sake, Casey."

"Because it isn't natural for women to have money?" she went on, pushing him. "Because it's not right for women to spend money on men?"

"Lay off," he said, giving up. "And maybe I'll let you buy me a Cadillac."

They stood up to go.

"I need to get a few things and find a room," she said.

"Listen," R.J. said, "I don't want you stuck in a hotel room somewhere. Hotels aren't safe."

"For Christ's sake, I've stayed in hotels before, R.J."

"Not with a maniac trying to kill you," he said. "There's a thousand ways to get at you in a hotel, and I can't cover them all."

She raised an eyebrow. "You have a better idea?"

"Yeah," he said, "I do."

CHAPTER 17

What's the matter?" asked R.J. "You don't like it?"

Casey stood just inside the door to his apartment, looking it over with pursed lips.

"It's fine," she said. "For you."

"Yeah, well, I couldn't get the decorators here this late in the day. Come on. You take the bedroom, I'll bunk out here on the couch."

She threw down an armload of shopping bags. They had stopped several times for her to get a few essentials, things she needed to replace the ruined wardrobe in her apartment. "I'll take the couch," she said.

"Oh, Christ," said R.J. "Here we go again."

She put both hands on her hips. "I'm not a delicate blushing flower, R.J. I'm a grown-up human being."

"A grown-up human being who's stubborn as two mules."

"Listen," she said. "This is your place—"

"No argument there."

"So why in the *hell* should you sleep on the couch in your own place?"

"I like the couch," he said. "The couch is very comfortable."

"Good. Then I'll sleep very well on it."

"Like hell you will. It's my couch, I'll sleep on it."

"Then I'll go stay in a goddamned hotel!" she yelled at him.

"You'll stay right here!" he yelled back.

They were toe to toe at this point, hollering into one another's face.

"I'm outta here!"

"You're staying! And you'll sleep in the goddamn bed!"

"Not alone, I won't!"

"Fine!" he said, and kissed her.

It was a short kiss. After just a few seconds she pushed him away, glared at him. "Fine," she said, and, putting a hand behind his head, she pulled his mouth down onto hers.

After a minute, he broke the kiss. "Don't think you're getting away with anything," he said, and kissed her again.

"I'm compromising," she said. "Which is more than you've ever done." Her voice was thick and heavy. He moved her over to the couch.

After that, neither of them said anything for a good long time.

For the first time since his first time, R.J. was swept away by a rising tide he could not control, could barely match.

They fell into each other on the couch, clawing and gasping like two wild animals. As R.J. worked to remove her battered business suit, he found Casey was ahead of him. She had his belt undone and his pants shagged down to his ankles while he was still puzzling out her buttons. She was with him, or ahead of him, every step of the way.

He decided to cut corners to catch up. Her pantyhose were already torn from her run-in with the wild cab. R.J. got a finger into a run at her knee and ripped upward, tearing the flimsy garment from her legs.

She bit his neck. He swore softly and bit her neck too. She moaned. He pulled at the neck of his shirt; buttons popped and he slid the blouse off her.

"Son of a bitch!" she gasped. "That was my only blouse!" She reached for the lapels of his shirt, in the center of his chest, and yanked; now his buttons flew off.

He popped the snaps on her bra and buried his head in her breasts. They were firm, nipples taut, and he crushed his mouth into them.

He heard her cry out softly and then felt her hands in the elastic band of his shorts. She yanked them down as far as she could, and her cool fingers found him.

R.J. twisted and slid his shorts and trousers to the floor, pushing them off with his feet so he could keep his hands on her. Then he slid his right hand down and worked her panties off, and they were both naked.

Their battle raged on. For a while she held the upper hand. R.J. saw everything through a red film; he thought he was going to bellow and ram his head into the wall.

Then, at just the right moment, she was suddenly soft and yielding, and as he entered her she dug her fingers into his back and arched forward to meet him.

Neither of them noticed when they slid off the couch and onto the hardwood floor.

Long minutes later, as they lay together, gasping for breath, R.J. realized they were eight feet away from the couch, in the middle of the room.

What have I got myself into? R.J. wondered. He felt

himself falling headfirst into something beyond his experience. He didn't know where it was going or what it would do to him, only that he couldn't stop now.

He looked at Casey. One arm was behind her head, supporting it. Her eyes were closed, her breathing even, and there was a small smile on her face.

A thin sheen of perspiration covered her face, neck, and breasts, adding a light gloss to the flush just beneath her skin.

I'm in deep shit, he thought.

But he had never seen anything half as beautiful before.

He sits across town in a quiet bar, a quiet man in a conservative business suit sipping his drink and thinking that he had never seen anything so beautiful in his life.

The way she had looked up at him, right before she died. Oh, she had seen him then. She had finally noticed him. He didn't seem so ordinary to her now—no, the face of your own death is never ordinary, is it?

She hadn't looked at him like that the first time, those many years ago. His big break. Yes, it actually had been his big break, come to think of it, but at the time—

It was a wonderful thing for a young actor, to win an audition for Belle Fontaine's new movie. To audition with Miss Fontaine in person.

He had gone into the studio office feeling important, worthy, for the first time since his parents' death. Past the guard at the gate. Past the secretaries. Into the conference room.

And she was there!

And she had looked him over, thoroughly, from head to toe, in just five seconds. And in that thrilling, velvety voice had said, "Get that horrible drab little creep out of here before I puke."

And he had been outside on the sidewalk, hypnotized by that wonderful voice, before he realized what she had said.

This had been before he came into his own, of course. Before he discovered the power he had, the greatness. And he had suffered.

Oh, how he had suffered. The years he spent inside a whiskey bottle. The growing desperation, even going to the AA meetings with those sad, pathetic weaklings hearing all about him. Hearing about his weakness. Listening to him, nodding.

Forgiving him.

Unforgivable. That they should judge him—hear his weakness and forgive him for it, like he really was just a drab, ordinary little rabbit—just like them!

He takes a long sip of his drink. That was so long ago. And he has found a way to pay off that debt too. Has found a way, at so many AA meetings, all over the country. A way to let the weaklings know he is not one of them. Not at all.

And that has passed many years, but still there has been the Big Debt, and the fact that he could do nothing about it had made him suffer.

All those years, all the suffering, all paid in full at last. In one glorious scene. Like all great moments in theater, it had just the right blend of sex and violence. By God, it had been good: the gun in his hand, Belle spread before him, the handsome coward trembling under her. It was his best so far, no doubt about it. . . .

So far. . . .

Because this next one will be better.

CHAPTER 18

R.J. woke up in his own bed with a feeling of strangeness to everything. The familiar surroundings just made it worse.

For a moment, between waking and sleeping, he couldn't understand what was different. The feel of the bed under him was right, was his. The smell—

He opened his eyes. Casey lay beside him, still asleep. The sweet, clean smell of her had drifted over to him, bringing him awake in a haze of desire without time or place.

Christ almighty, he thought, looking her over. She had kicked the covers off and lay there completely naked. R.J. felt himself growing hard and shook his head. All night long, and I still want her.

He ran his eyes over her, marveling at her flawless skin and silky contours. He had worked his way down to her toes and halfway back up again when he became aware that she was awake.

"You going to do something about it, or just look?" she said.

"I didn't want to wake you up."

"R.J., there's one way you can always wake me up."

He reached a hand out and cupped her breast.

"Yup, that's the way," she said, pulling him down.

———————— ◆ ————————

When R.J. woke up the second time she was gone from the bed. He heard the shower running.

He lay with his hands behind his head, thinking things over. Sure, she was smart, attractive as hell, fearless, competent, and terrific in the sack. Why should that make him feel like his brains had turned to mush?

Maybe he was just vulnerable now, with his mother's death to deal with. That would explain how she had gotten so deeply into him so fast: His defenses were down, something like this could blindside him, get under his skin. That was probably it.

But whatever it was, it was bothering him. He should have it out in the open with her, see what she was thinking, and get on with it.

A few minutes later, Casey came out of the bathroom. She had wrapped his bath towel around her and had another towel turbaned around her hair.

She moved quickly through the room and out into the living room. R.J. heard her rustling through her packages, fishing out new clothes.

She came back in and began to dress.

"Hey," he said. "Casey. Come here."

She looked up and flashed him a neutral smile. "I'm in kind of a hurry, R.J. Running late." She shrugged into a handsome, conservative business outfit.

"Listen," he said, "I was thinking—"

"R.J., I have an interview at the World Trade Cen-

tcr in forty-five minutes. Save the thought, all right?"
And she moved back into the bathroom, clutching a
hairbrush and her new makeup kit.

"Sure," he said to her back. "It'll keep."

The change in her was so complete she might have
been a different person. Now she was all business, a
hard-shelled career woman with no time for tender-
ness.

And maybe that's the real her, R.J. thought. Maybe
last night *she* was feeling vulnerable after her brush with
death. Maybe she wasn't at all like the woman he was
falling for, and for her it had just been a way to thumb
her nose at death, something that didn't mean a thing
in the light of day.

So maybe it ended here.

The thought left him cold and empty. There had
been a lot of women in R.J.'s life, but none had ever
taken him over like this, and after only one night. He
already needed her; not just for sex, although that had
been great, about the best ever.

He needed her for more, for things he couldn't even
put into words. He needed her, and it made him un-
comfortable as hell to need somebody like that.

I really am in trouble, he thought.

He dragged himself out of bed and into the kitchen.
Casey was standing with the refrigerator door open,
looking dubiously at the contents.

"Time for coffee?" he asked her.

"Uh, no, not really. Do you have any juice?"

"There's some Tang in the cupboard," he said help-
fully.

She shuddered. "Thanks, I'd rather not." She closed
the refrigerator. "I'll get something on the way downtown."

She started for the door.

"Hang on a sec," he said to her back.

She turned around with an expression of impatient politeness. "Yes?"

"You'll need a key. For tonight. In case I'm not here."

"All right," she said. He went into the bedroom and found his spare keys. She didn't ask him where he was going to be.

"Here you go," he said. "I'll see you later." He leaned forward to give her a kiss, but she had already turned and was out the door.

R.J. dragged himself through a shower. Casey had used up most of the hot water, so the shower was not as long as he would have liked. When he got out, there were no towels left either. He blotted himself half dry with a towel that was heavy with water and Casey's smell.

He got dressed in a worn pair of brown corduroys and a tan chamois shirt from L.L. Bean. The shirt stuck to his damp back.

He combed his hair and went into the kitchen for a cup of coffee. As the hot brown liquid started to move through his veins, R.J. could feel his brain coming awake.

It was after ten o'clock. There was nothing he could do about Casey, not right now. So he put her out of his mind and concentrated on the killer.

He knew damned little about the guy. Just that he was slick and quick and good at disguises. He could add to that a couple of guesses: Casey's hunch about the guy acting things out, for instance.

He thought about that for a minute. Was it possible that the guy wasn't acting out—but *acting*?

He turned the idea over a few times. It made sense. It explained his skill with disguises. And it could be a connection to Belle, the way he knew her, the reason he had wanted to kill her. She hadn't been any kind of angel, especially in her early career in Hollywood. She'd been drinking a lot back then, maybe trying to keep up with his old man, and she was a mean drunk.

Maybe she'd said or done something to the killer back then, something that festered and grew into a psychotic need to kill her. Actors were flaky at best; who knew what might push one of them over the edge?

An actor; why not? It would explain the makeup and the motive. It also gave him a place to start.

R.J. rooted out his battered telephone directory from the small table in the living room where he kept his phone and answering machine. He thumbed through, looking for one particular number. Yup. He still had it.

Arthur Drake. His mother's old agent in Hollywood. Arthur had retired years ago, but if anyone had a line on who might have a reason to come out of the past and kill Belle, it would be Arthur. His memory for names and faces was legendary. And he'd always had a kind word and a piece of hard candy for young R.J. too.

He dialed. After eleven rings, a man picked up.

"Hello?" came a weak and quavery voice on the far end.

"Hello, Arthur, it's me. R.J. Brooks."

"Who is it?" said the old voice.

"R.J. Brooks. Belle Fontaine's son." He was almost shouting.

There was a long pause. R.J. could hear the old man fumbling with the receiver. "Is it R.J.?" he finally said.

"Yes, that's right!"

"Oh," said Arthur. "Well, how are you, my boy?"

"I'm fine, Arthur, how are you?!"

"You don't have to shout," Arthur said, and R.J. could hear a faint echo of the man's old-time urbanity in his voice. "I can hear you perfectly well now."

"Oh. Well, great, how are you, Arthur?"

"I'm old and deaf, but otherwise as well as can be expected," he said. "Please let me offer my sincerest condolences."

"Thank you," R.J. said.

"Your mother was a wonderful woman, R.J. I know you did not get along famously of late, but never forget what a remarkable talent she was. Truly remarkable, and we shall all miss her terribly."

"I know, Arthur. Thanks a lot."

"Well," said the old man briskly. "By my best recollection, it has been thirteen years since I've spoken to you. To what do I owe this call?"

"It's about Belle's murder. I need some help."

"Indeed."

"I got an idea that the killer might be an actor. Somebody who knew her professionally."

"Ah-hah." R.J. could almost hear the gears whirring in the old man's head, a stack of cards dropping into the slot. "Have you anything more than that?"

"No, I'm sorry, that's it. There's nothing definite, but it would make a lot of sense if that's how it was."

"All right then. How can I help?"

"Arthur, you were her agent for a lot of those years out there."

"All the good ones, my boy. And some not quite so good."

"I remember," R.J. said. "I was wondering if anything stuck in your mind, any incident where somebody might have wanted to hurt her. It wouldn't have to be anything definite, just somebody who got mad at her, or whatever."

"Well, R.J. I can think of ten or fifteen very specific death threats Belle received."

"Jesus Christ!" R.J. exploded. "Are you serious?"

"Oh, yes," the old man assured him. "Your mother was very demanding, like so many great creative artists. That led to an awful lot of friction. And as I say, at least a dozen times it led to somewhat more."

"Who were they, Arthur?"

The old man laughed. "Almost a Who's Who of Hollywood, old chap. Names you wouldn't believe if I told you. Of course," he said, a note of regret creeping into his voice, "most of the really interesting ones are dead now. So many dead." He sighed.

"This could be important, Arthur. Can you check and let me know of any that might still be alive? And maybe still holding a grudge?"

"Of course I shall, dear boy. I would do a great deal more for your mother, or for you. And in fact, with your illustrious bloodlines, which I believe show strongly in your looks, if you should reconsider your career options I can still—"

"No thanks, Arthur. Not for me. But I'd appreciate it if you can find something on this thing."

"Like winged Mercury from great Zeus, I go," said Arthur.

"Thanks, Arthur. I'll call you."

"God bless you, my boy," the old man said and hung up.

Ten or fifteen, R.J. thought. *Holy Christ.* He'd been worried that he would find just another dead end, and he guessed he should be grateful there was a chance of a lead, but this . . . He shook his head. It was looking like a miracle she'd lived as long as she had.

He went back into the kitchen for another cup of coffee. As he sipped he thought some more. He could wait for Arthur to come up with something, but that could take days. Anyway, that wasn't his style. If he was going to sit around, he'd start thinking about Casey, so he might as well get out and do something.

That's half a decision, he thought. Now, exactly what should I do?

It occurred to him as he finished his coffee: his mother's journals. He could go at the same problem from the other end. She would surely have made some mention of death threats, run-ins, things like that.

He rinsed his cup out in the sink, grabbed his coat, and headed out.

CHAPTER 19

R.J. took a cab over to his mother's apartment—*his* apartment now—and spent the ride thinking he was taking too many cabs lately. He wondered what that meant.

Maybe it went with the apartment. People who lived at that kind of building took cabs. Or limos. And hired somebody to walk their poodle and pick up the droppings.

Belle had never had a poodle, he thought with approval. Or a cat, or a cockatiel, or even a goldfish, for that matter.

The cab pulled up in front of the building. If you didn't know much about New York you might walk right by the place without a second look, and that's pretty much the way the residents wanted it.

But if you knew the warning signs, you could almost smell the mink inside. This was a high-class place, in the old-fashioned, lunch at the Algonquin sense. The apartments inside could not be bought. There were almost never vacancies. You just about had to inherit them.

Christ, he'd have to sell the place or something. It wasn't his style. It just wasn't *him*.

But it *was* his mother. When he thought about that, R.J. didn't know if he could bring himself to sell the apartment.

The cab pulled up in front of the building. While R.J. was paying the driver, Tony, the doorman, opened the cab's door.

"Mr. Brooks," he said. "Gladda see you."

R.J. stepped out. "Thanks, Tony. How's it going?"

Tony shrugged and waved the cab on. "Can't complain. How's about you, Mr. Brooks?"

"I could complain plenty, but nobody listens."

Tony gave him a polite laugh and ushered him inside.

The elevator always worked in this building. And it never smelled like pee or cheap disinfectant. R.J. wondered if maybe he shouldn't move here after all. Sure, he thought. And I can live off the interest on my inheritance. Learn ballroom dancing, grow a little mustache. Get a Pekingese.

His sour thoughts ended when he pushed open the door to his mother's apartment. He closed the door and stood there in the small foyer for a minute. The place still felt so much like his mother that he half expected her to come striding down the hallway, calling, "Darling! We're late," as she tossed her hair back and shrugged into her coat.

He shook his head. She was gone for good, and he still wasn't sure who she had been.

He went into the study and pulled out a stack of journals.

Because he didn't know where to start, or even what

to look for, R.J. figured it didn't much matter. He had as good a chance to hit it random as by planning. So he started reading from a time about a year after his father's death.

He opened it to the first page and was shocked at the handwriting. Instead of the neat, evenly spaced spider tracks he was used to, this was a shaky scrawl, going up and down the page in a series of uneven lurches.

He was jolted again as he began to read.

I'd give anything for a drink. It's all I can think about. That beautiful, golden liquid, floating so serenely in the glass, sliding over my tongue and down my throat like liquid fire, lighting me up when it hits with its warm, wise glow—God help me, I don't know if I can be this strong.

If only I had someone to lean on—but I don't. There's no one, nothing, nowhere to turn but inward to myself, and I'm not sure I like what I see there when I look.

Arthur has been calling twice a day, and so has that horrible little weasel from the studio. At least I know what *he* wants.

And I know what I want too—something to drink, anything. I've even been looking with longing at the lighter fluid.

But I have to beat this before I can face any of them—and I don't know if I can.

I've never felt so alone. . . .

So she had tried to kick by herself. God, he knew that feeling. And he hadn't been drinking as long and as hard as she had when he did it. He had just barely pulled himself out of alcoholism. For his mother to fight it like that . . .

Of course, he had known she had stopped drinking.

At the time it didn't seem like a big deal; okay, she stopped drinking, so what?

But to read about it like this, to get a step-by-step account of her struggle—somehow that brought it home to him in a way nothing had before.

R.J. flipped ahead. About halfway through the volume the handwriting steadied again. He went back a few pages and started reading.

Well, if anybody asks me, the answer is yes. I *do* know Bill W.

I met him last night, in the fellowship hall at Bel Air Presbyterian Church.

So his mother had gone to Alcoholics Anonymous. That was not really a surprise, anyway. He'd known that for years. And why shouldn't she have gone? The thing worked. Just because he had been too mule-headed to try it didn't mean anything. He hadn't tried it *because* he knew it worked. Had to prove to himself he didn't need anybody or anything, that he was stronger than the need.

Okay, he'd proved it. But for his mother, it must have been even harder to go, to ask for help, to expose herself like that. Nowadays any celebrity with half a brain does detox as the first step in their professional comeback. They're probably put through it by their publicity people. But back then, when Belle did it, a whisper of that kind of trouble killed careers.

He read some more.

Don't know why it should be a surprise to *me*, but to see some of the faces there and pretend not to know them, when everyone in the *world* would know them anywhere—These are marquis names of the first order, sitting in their folding chairs and sipping their coffee like it was the most natural thing in the world.

But anyway, it certainly made me feel a bit better. I'm not alone.

I guess that's one of the strong points of these little get-togethers, letting all of us know we're not alone, that others just like us are facing the same problem. It's funny how much that one small thing seems to help.

R.J. could picture the gathering, all those famous names in one place, like one of those fantasy sketches from the fan magazines; lunch at the MGM commissary.

Of course, this would have a slightly different title: AA Meeting of the Stars.

And his mother had fit right in, had *made* herself fit in.

Or had she? He flipped ahead and read on.

And here I thought I was getting into something that didn't relate to career at all. I certainly won't make that mistake again. I can't understand why that evil old bitch would snub me like that. After all, she was pleasant enough at the AA meeting.

Perhaps that's why—she doesn't want to admit to herself, in daylight, that she goes. So anyone who sees her there is poison.

Well, considering how her last picture did, she won't be able to keep that attitude in place forever.

And considering how hard it is for me to get my next picture off the ground, how long can I keep pretending that anyone wants to see me on the screen?

I'm quite sure I'm too young to be a has-been, but it's not up to me. I always felt just a little like I

was faking it, like I didn't really belong. Maybe
that shows. Maybe the public can see that.

Maybe I am all washed up. . . .

R.J. read the volume through and then another. He
found himself liking this person, admiring her strength,
her willingness to struggle, her vulnerability. He began
to like her so much that when he remembered it was
his mother, he was startled into putting the book down.

I blew it, he thought. I really blew it. I never got to
know her until it was too late. And I never let her get to
know me. Maybe because I don't know who I am.

Maybe all the things I thought were wrong with her
were really just the way I looked at her because of what
was wrong with *me*. Maybe it's *my* life that's a mess, he
thought. Because he was pretty sure he didn't have the
kind of sharp, stubborn spunk his mother showed in
her journals.

Sure, he was stubborn too. Pig-headed, in fact. But
he had used his mulishness to keep her away, while she
was using hers to keep trying to reach him. Even after
he had pushed her away with all his strength, she was
strong enough to keep pushing back, trying to get
closer to her only son.

Whatever else she had been, his mother hadn't been
a quitter.

R.J. spent the rest of the day reading the journals,
with long pauses between volumes. As he finished one
he'd set it down and think, adding up what he was
learning about his mother and contrasting it with what
he knew about himself.

By the time it got dark he had reached a couple of
conclusions.

The first was that if the killer had come out of his
mother's past, she hadn't been aware of him; at least
there was no mention, no hint, in the journals of any-

thing that might lead to a name or a suspicious incident.

The second realization was that he owed her one.

He hadn't done much with his life so far. He now realized that all his mother's awkward calls and attempts at pushing him were aimed at helping him toward that goal. He'd shoved her away, distanced himself as much as possible, made it incredibly difficult for her to call or see him.

Okay, she'd been a lousy mother when he was a kid. But she'd gotten herself sober and tried to make up for it. It was his fault that she hadn't managed it.

Was it too late? Could he make it up by salvaging something from his life before he was too far gone down that dirt road he stuck to so stubbornly?

He could carve a pretty good career out of what he had done already. And take over raising his son. God knew the kid needed a father right now. And then—

R.J. thought about Casey. He wondered if what bothered him most about her was that he was ready to make a commitment to her, and he wasn't sure how she felt about him.

He thought of all the times some weepy-eyed woman had tried to sink her long red nails into his back and hold him down long enough to get a ring through his nose. How he'd always managed to laugh it off, wriggle away to the next one. How secretly pleased he'd always been with his fancy footwork.

And now there was Casey, keeping him wondering, off-balance, the same way.

Well, buster, he thought, the shoe's on the other foot now. And it doesn't fit so good. In fact, it hurts like hell.

He closed up the apartment and headed for home.

CHAPTER 20

Casey was waiting for him when he got back to his apartment.

"R.J.!" She seemed pleased to see him, even planted a kiss on his face.

"Hi, doll," R.J. said, sliding in the door.

"What a great day," she said. "I nailed my interview, got some stuff on tape that is major league. Hot damn, I'm good! This is absolutely going to jump-start my career."

And she was off toward the kitchen, leaving R.J. to wonder if she was really glad to see him, or just happy to have an audience to hear about a good career move.

R.J. followed her into the kitchen, already feeling glum. On top of the emotional roller-coaster ride that reading his mother's journals had put him through, he wasn't up to another round of trying to figure out Casey.

He stopped just inside the door, his nose twitching at the strange new odors.

Several pots were bubbling on the stove. "What's the smell?"

She flashed a smile. "Ratatouille."

"Rat-what?"

"It's a vegetable casserole," she said. "To celebrate my day."

He shook his head. "You celebrate with vegetables? Whatever happened to steak?"

"It's good," she said. "You'll like it." There was an "or else" hidden in her voice, but she was smiling as she shook a wooden cooking spoon at him.

"No meat on the side?" he asked.

She shook her head. "No meat."

"Not even a hot dog?"

"R.J. . . ." she said with naked warning in her voice.

He sank woefully into one of the straight-backed kitchen chairs. "Jesus, I'm glad one of us is having a good day. No meat."

Actually, the stuff didn't taste too bad, and there was plenty of it, served on a bed of wild rice. R.J. wasn't hungry when he finished eating, but he felt like he should be.

Casey washed hers down with two glasses of white wine, a little dismayed when she found out he didn't drink. "You don't mind if I do?" She had asked.

"Hell, no, I like the smell."

"Then why don't you drink?"

He showed her some teeth. "I like the taste too. In fact, I like everything about it. I like it a little too much, so I stay away from it."

"But you don't mind if I do? Because it's not a big deal for me."

"It's not a big deal for me either," he told her. "Go for it."

"If you're sure," she said.

"I'm sure, for Christ's sake. Cheers, bottoms up, *skal, salud, prost, nostrovya.* Drink, already."

"Don't mind if I do," she said.

They sat across from each other at his awful old kitchen table. R.J. watched the muscles work in her neck and jaw as she ate. Funny, he thought. Eating never looked elegant before.

Casey looked so good, in fact, that for a long moment R.J. forgot to eat. Then he realized that she was staring at him.

"What?" she asked.

"Nothing," he said and put his face back in the plate. But when he was sure she wouldn't notice, he snuck a few more looks at her.

After dinner R.J. trotted out his espresso machine, an old gift from his mother he had used maybe twice, and made cappuccino.

Rummaging in the refrigerator for milk, he noticed that Casey had been shopping. The whole damned box was filled with juices, vegetables, and fruits. And no meat, he thought to himself.

As he served Casey a small earthenware cup of cappuccino, she raised one perfectly shaped dark eyebrow at him. "Gorgeous," she said, nodding to the cup, with its light dusting of spice atop the stiff peak of milk. She sipped the coffee and added, "And it tastes as good as it looks. You do this often?"

"Every time you celebrate."

After they had finished coffee they moved onto the couch in the living room. She rattled on some more about how good her day had been.

"But Jesus, listen to me," she finally said. "I've been talking my ass off." She looked at him accusingly. "And you haven't said a thing to slow me down, damn it."

"That's my fault?" R.J. asked with astonishment. "Damn, I always take the heat for *not* letting a woman talk, and now I'm getting both barrels because I do."

"You should have stopped me. Told me I was talking too much. I *hate* a woman who babbles on and on. I never do this, it's just I really was excited about this interview and I lost it for a minute. But I'm not a chatterbox."

"There you go again," he said.

She slugged him on the arm. "All right, asshole," she said. "So tell me about your day."

R.J. hesitated. He wanted to tell her about reading his mother's journals and the things he had discovered—about her and about himself. But as he took a breath to begin, he found he couldn't say any of the important things.

He really did want to tell her. He wanted to bring her closer by sharing what he was learning about himself. As his lover, she might want to know, and knowing might bind them together.

But she was a reporter too—and which person would hear these intimate confessions, the lover or the reporter?

He didn't know. And because he had no idea what their relationship really was, he couldn't figure it out and couldn't really open up to her any more.

"Oh," he said at last, "I tried to run down a few leads. I talked to Belle's old agent, out on the Coast."

Casey leaned forward, her eyes sparkling. "Did he know about any threats on Belle's life?"

He gave her a bleak smile. "Ten or fifteen."

She looked stunned. "Oh."

"But he's going to check around, see if anybody who made a threat is still alive, in a position to do anything."

R.J. lapsed into a moody silence. Casey let him, saying nothing for fifteen minutes.

R.J. sank deeper into his thoughts. His mother's life and her death, his own life, the killer, Casey—it all made an unsettling porridge in his mind. He couldn't even come up with one piece of it solid enough to let him think about it. Instead, his brain just circled around the chunks, over and over.

He was so far away inside himself that it was several minutes before he noticed what Casey was doing.

When it finally occurred to him, he glanced down into his lap. Her hand was there, reaching inside his open zipper.

He looked up at her face.

"Cat got your tongue?" she asked him.

He tried to speak, couldn't, cleared his throat, and tried again. "That's not my tongue," he said.

She moved closer. "I'm not actually a cat, either," she said.

She leaned her head down upon his shoulder and slipped a hand inside his shirt. He could feel her hot breath on his neck.

"Cheer up," she said, her voice husky.

For a while, he did.

The telephone rang a little after midnight. R.J. came awake on the first ring and carefully slid Casey's weight off his chest before fumbling for the receiver.

"Hello?"

"Que va, hombre?" said the voice on the other end.

"Uncle Hank, where are you?"

"At Dulles. I'm about to get on the shuttle for Kennedy. I think I have some things that will interest you."

"What time do you get in?"

"In about two hours. Is your couch free?"

R.J. looked over at Casey, who half opened her eyes, then rolled over, turning her perfect back to him. "Sure it is. Come on over."

"Hey, *chico*, no karate chops this time, huh?"

"All right. I'll be waiting for you."

"With some coffee, I hope. *Hasta luego*, R.J."

R.J. hung up. He looked at Casey's back in the dimness of the room. He put out a hand and ran it lightly along her silky spine. She shivered lightly, said, "Mmm," but did not wake up.

They had spent an hour and a half in passionate lovemaking that was half combat. In spite of that, or perhaps because of it, he still didn't know where he stood with her.

He had never been with a woman who ran so hot and cold. There were times when he was sure she was nuts about him. There were other times when he was just as sure she was only using him to kill time. It was starting to make him crazy, and he didn't have a clue what to do about it.

He moved his hand up to her side and ran it down over the rich swell of her hip. Whatever was going on, he didn't want it to stop.

R.J. got up and threw on his clothes. Then he went to the kitchen and made a pot of coffee.

CHAPTER 21

"This is terrible coffee," Henry Portillo said, halfway through his third cup. "And I speak as an expert. You should taste what the *Federales* call coffee."

"What's wrong with the coffee?" R.J. asked him. He was slightly miffed; coffee was important to him, and this stuff came from fancy beans.

Hank made a face. "Too strong. Also, you must have used some kind of fancy European coffee bean. And then, this New York water is terrible, R.J. So naturally the coffee is all wrong."

"You should have brought your own goddamned water, then. Along with the goddamned tortillas," R.J. told him.

Hank raised an eyebrow. "You didn't like the tortillas? You ate enough of them."

R.J. opened his mouth to say something back and stopped. Instead, he looked long and hard at Henry Portillo. There were new lines on Uncle Hank's face, lines that would not go away with a good night's sleep. And they looked like they were brought on by more than just the years.

"What's with you, Uncle Hank? I haven't heard you complain this much in fifteen years."

The older man raised a hand to his face and rubbed the bridge of his nose.

"I'm tired, boy. I'm tired of chasing bad guys and catching lawyers." He shook his head. "For too many years. *Demasiado.*"

R.J. could see real signs of age in his uncle for the first time. True, his hair had been slowly turning white for many years—but that had just added character. Now, for the first time, Uncle Hank looked old.

R.J. was sure it was not just cop burnout, no matter what Portillo might say. It was the strain of Belle's death. He had loved her, and that love had gone unresolved and even unspoken.

A lot like R.J.'s love, in fact.

"Have some more terrible coffee, Uncle Hank," R.J. said, hoping to throw off the mood.

Portillo made a face. "What I need is some *huevos rancheros.*"

R.J. grinned. "You're nothing but a *tio taco,* Uncle Hank."

He nodded. "That may be," he said. "But when I make it, it is a very *good* taco."

R.J. drained his coffee cup and set the cup down. "And when I make coffee, it's very good coffee," he said. "What have you got for me?"

Hank flipped a thick manila folder onto the kitchen table.

"This," he said. He opened the folder and started to riffle through the thick stack of papers inside it.

"As you know, I've been down at Quantico, working with the FBI's Behavioral Science Unit." He waved a hand. "It's just, you know. *Una cosa politica.* One of the things the LAPD sends me on every now and then. To keep the Department up to date, to network with other departments. Like that.

"Anyway, I got some use out of the computer there, in my spare time. I ran their program for myself. I fed in everything we know about the killer, most of what we guess, details of the crime scene, that sort of thing. And the computer developed a profile of the killer."

R.J. felt his pulse quicken. In spite of the lateness of the hour, the lack of sleep, his confused emotions, this was something he could focus on. This made everything else unimportant.

"Let's have it," he said.

"Not so fast," Portillo told him. "This is by no means complete, R.J. At the moment it's kind of a patchwork outline, no more. It's a starting place."

"I don't care if it's only a matchbook from the Holiday Inn," R.J. said. "It's more than we've had before, and more than the cops have. Let's see it."

A sleep-filled voice came from behind them. "Let's see what?"

Henry Portillo whirled out of his chair and faced the direction of the new voice in a half crouch, one hand under his jacket for his gun before R.J. stopped him.

"At ease, Uncle Hank. She's one of us."

Casey stood in the doorway, wrapped in R.J.'s bathrobe. Her hair was tousled, and there were some traces of sleep in her voice, but her eyes were clear and alert. She looked fantastic, R.J. thought.

Henry straightened slowly. "Of course I know Miss Wingate," he said carefully. "But I didn't know—"

R.J. grinned. Uncle Hank was still a little bit of a prude, even after all those years on the LAPD. R.J. knew that the older man, who was visibly blushing beneath his dark, desert tan, had always been bothered by his "nephew's" tendency to stray from the straight and narrow.

"You didn't know she was so low class and tasteless as to show up in the middle of the night wearing my bathrobe."

"I—That's—" The older man spluttered helplessly, caught between gallantry and morality.

"Well, relax, Uncle Hank. The killer made a try for Casey, trashed her place completely. She's staying with me for a while. That's all." And as he said it, he wondered how true it was.

Casey stepped forward and held her hand out, not realizing—or not caring—that the gesture caused the bathrobe to open a little more than was strictly proper. Portillo's blush deepened and he looked away, even as he took her hand.

"R.J. has told me an awful lot about you, Mr. Portillo," she said.

"Well, that's, I," he said, trying to recover. "I'm sure most of it is lies and exaggerations, Miss Wingate."

"I'm sure it must be," said Casey. "I don't see a big red *S* on your chest."

"Casey's been working on this with me," R.J. said, as much to have something to say to cover the older man's embarrassment as anything else.

"Oh," said Portillo, still flustered. "Oh, well then." He gave R.J. a glance that was not exactly full of approval.

"Relax, Uncle Hank," R.J. told him. "She's legit, I promise."

"Well. Very well," Portillo said. But he remained standing.

R.J. laughed again; just one short bark. He was enjoying this. "Sit down, Casey. He won't sit until you do."

Casey smiled and moved to the closest chair. "A real

old-fashioned gentleman," she said. "That's a pleasant change." She sat down gracefully, this time remembering to hold the robe closed.

"Okay, Uncle Hank," R.J. said. "Let's have it."

"Yes," Portillo said. He stepped back to his chair and sat down again. He slid a pair of rimless half-glasses from a black leather case, put them on his nose, and paged carefully through the file.

"All right then," he said and began to read down a page he pulled from the stack.

"The first thing I did, after I fed in everything we had, was to ask the program to establish a pattern in the M.O. Then I asked if there were unsolved matches in the computer's data banks."

"Did you find one?" R.J. butted in, excited.

Hank looked at him bleakly over the top of the paper. "I found a dozen," he said, holding up a thick printout. "Chicago, Atlanta, San Diego, Houston, Sacramento—all over the damn country."

"But they all fit the pattern?" Casey asked.

Portillo shrugged. "They seem to. But we have to ask what good it does us for them to fit a pattern if the pattern is popping up everywhere."

"Sure," said R.J. "It's more likely that the information you entered wasn't detailed enough, and you got the computer to spit out a whole crop of different psychos, all over the country."

"That's possible," said Portillo, nodding.

"What about the dates? Do any of them conflict?" Casey asked, leaning forward to look at the printout.

Portillo looked at her with approval. "Good for you, Miss Wingate. It took me almost a full day before I asked that question. No, none of the dates conflict. In theory it *could* have been the same person, acting at different times in different spots."

"But what do all those cities have in common?" Casey mused.

R.J. shrugged. "They're American cities, all medium to large in size. So maybe the killer needs to stay in areas that offer something you can't get in the sticks."

"Like what?" Portillo asked.

R.J. grinned at him. "Like a good cup of coffee, Uncle Hank. How the hell would I know, like what?"

"The important thing is, if we have that many kills we have a better chance of finding some clue at one of them," Casey said.

"Sure," R.J. said, "*if* they're all the same guy. If they're not, anything we find might take us on a wild goose chase."

"The local cops have been over every one of those crime scenes," Portillo said. "They found no more than what we did. A bizarre and grotesque scene, a handful of Polaroids—that's it."

"Look," said Casey, "we know more about this killer than all the local cops put together. Let's go through each one of these and see if they add up."

"How would you like us to decide, Miss Wingate?" Portillo asked her with a touch of polite derision.

She snorted. "Call me 'Casey.' And cut the crap."

Portillo flinched slightly. He had never gotten used to having women use words like *crap*. "Very well. *Casey*. How shall we decide?"

"R.J. and I have both been over three of these kills in the New York area. I think we have a feel for the guy's style, even in the absence of evidence. And don't," she said, cutting off the older man's objections, "give me any shit about woman's intuition, all right? Any half-decent cop works hunches all the time, and you know it."

Portillo shook his head and said something in Spanish under his breath.

Casey turned to R.J. "What did he say?"

R.J. laughed. "You don't want to know. Let's just do it, okay?"

For the next few hours they sat together at the rickety kitchen table, hunched over the pages, passing them back and forth, marking a few spots, occasionally commenting to each other.

When they were done, the sun was coming up. They had a stack of nine cases they agreed were the work of the same killer, three uncertain, and one they threw out.

"All right then," said Portillo, tapping the sheaf of papers on the table to get the edges even. "I will run these nine back into the computer and see what we come up with."

He placed the papers back into the manila folder and closed it.

"And now," Portillo said, standing up and stretching, "I believe there is just time for *huevos rancheros* before I must catch the shuttle."

CHAPTER 22

R.J. stopped in at his office at noon. As he opened the outer door, Wanda met him with a look of cold petulance.

"What's that face?" he asked her.

"Nothing, I'm sure," she said. "After all, you're the boss. You don't even have to come in to the office if you don't want to. You have an employee to take messages and run the office. Just stay in bed all day, if that's what the two of you want to do."

R.J. stifled a laugh. "Is there more?"

"You're darn right, there's more," she said, not even pretending to be civil now. "Boss, I've worked here for *three years*—and not *once* in all that time did you see fit to tell me who you *really* are! R.J. *Brooks*—what a laugh! I have a right to know who I'm working for, at least, and I *thought* there was a little more to the relationship than that, but if you—"

R.J. put his hands to his ears in an attempt to block

out the torrent that was pouring out. "Whoa, whoa, for Christ's sake, slow down. Jesus, Wanda!"

"—can't even give me one civil word of explanation, even when I *ask* you right out, then all I can say—"

R.J. stepped over to Wanda and placed a hand gently but firmly over her mouth.

"There's lots of stuff I've never told you," he said. "And I never will. That doesn't mean anything. You're my friend, and I'm glad you work here, but my private business is private, got it?"

She made muffled sounds of protest and looked poison at him.

"Now, I'm going to tell you this one time, and one time only. Yes, Belle Fontaine was my mother. I've spent the last ten years running from that. I never mentioned it because I didn't want to think about it myself. I've been trying to forget it. I thought it wasn't important.

"I was wrong about that. I'm sorry she had to get killed for me to figure it out, but that's water under the bridge. All that matters now is finding the guy who did it, okay?"

Once again she made a muffled noise, but not a violent one this time, and the look in her eyes had softened.

R.J. nodded. "Good. I'm going to take my hand away now, and I don't want to hear another word about this, all right?"

He slowly took his hand away.

Wanda stared at him, watching him inch his hand back. When he finally dropped it to his side, she said one word.

"Asshole." She returned to her desk. "Here's a list of your calls. You'll notice most of them are from Tina Burkette. She wants to 'Finalize the schedule of payments,' which I think means the hot tub again."

"Oh, brother."

"Uh-huh. Well, you got yourself into hot water, you can get yourself out."

"Pretty funny. Anything else?"

"A couple of other calls, nothing important: Gloria wants to see you. Your accountant called; he says he needs about four hours of your time—"

"Jesus Christ," R.J. said. "I don't spend four hours with him in five years!"

Wanda gave him a mean smile. "You will, now you're rich. I think you'll be spending a lot of time with Fender, Bean, and Weinstock."

"Hell, I can't do it. Bean has breath that could knock a vulture off an outhouse."

"It can wait until next week," Wanda said sweetly.

"Quit your damn gloating. What else?"

"Why do you think there's more?"

"Isn't there?"

"Yes. A handful of prospective clients. I told them you weren't taking any new jobs right now."

"One of these days, you'll go too far and I'll spank you."

"Promises, promises," she said, and R.J. went on into his office, letting her have the last word.

R.J. spent about forty minutes with some routine paperwork and then called Wanda in to dictate a letter.

She settled into the chair beside his desk, smoothing down her skirt over her crossed legs.

"Ready, boss," she said, poised with her pen and pad.

"Dear Mrs. Burkette," R.J. began, sticking a cigar in his mouth as he leaned back in his chair, almost to a full horizontal.

"Oh, boy," muttered Wanda, "here it comes."

"Sorry I have not responded to your recent calls. I've been away from the office on a very complicated and time-consuming new case. Paragraph. I can't see that we have anything further to finalize, but if I have overlooked some small detail, please feel free to discuss it with my confidential assistant, Wanda Groz."

"Thanks a *lot*," said Wanda.

"You're welcome. Paragraph. I hope you are as satisfied with the outcome of my work for you as I am. If I can be of any future assistance, please don't hesitate to call. Sincerely, et cetera."

"Old Mr. Fuller's got nothing on you, boss," Wanda said, slapping shut her notebook.

"How's that?"

She gave him a shark's smile, which meant she was back to normal again. "You give a great brush-off," she said, and she swished out of his office.

R.J. leaned back in his chair again, letting his mind drift.

He thought about Casey for a good long time. He still didn't know what to make of her hot-and-cold act. The hot was the best he'd ever had. But the cold was killing him.

He threw the soggy, mangled cigar at the trash can. With an effort he put Casey out of his head and thought instead about what Henry Portillo had learned about the killer. Chicago, Atlanta, San Diego, Houston, Sacramento: all over the damned country.

What the hell did any of them have in common?

The man sitting in the dim, midtown bar knows the answer to that one. In fact, he knows the answer to a lot of puzzling questions.

For instance: How much horrible, permanently mutilating pain can a human being stand before going completely mad?

That's one of his favorite questions.

He asks it frequently.

In Chicago, Atlanta, San Diego, Houston, Sacramento. And of course, Manhattan.

He loves to explore the answer to that one. It is always different. He never gets tired of helping someone stretch beyond that red line they thought marked the end of the world and show them, oh no, there's more.

See? You can go just a little bit further.

See? A little further again.

Of course, they all do go mad, sooner or later. At that point they're no longer very much fun.

The woman had surprised him. She had been much stronger than he had thought she would be. She had lasted for several hours.

Remarkable, really. The reserves in the woman. Quite as powerful as anything she had ever done onscreen.

And he had been magnificent too. Of course, he had no movie roles to compare his performance to, but he had known. It had been the performance of his life.

Better than anything he had ever done before—in Chicago, Atlanta, San Diego, Houston, and Sacramento. All the miserable, half-sophisticated hick towns where he'd gotten dinner theater roles.

All the moldy hotel rooms, the dim and uncomprehending audiences, interested only in two-for-one drinks and pawing at each other.

And he had to go through with it, all the hundreds of performances of Barefoot in the Park, The Fantasticks, Camelot, The Owl and the Pussycat. *Nothing ever changed; the shows the same, the other actors performing in the same way, saying the same shallow, stupid, self-centered things, even the towns the same after a while.*

No relief from the horrifying, blurry murk of the whole existence. No relief at all—except when The Feeling comes and he plays out a scene as he has scripted it himself.

The quickened pulse as he spots a potential scene partner and knows, Yes, that one. The delicious delay as he follows them home from the AA meeting, planning the scene, wondering how it would be, hoping he's found a partner with real talent.

And then it would happen. And always just a little disappointment afterward, when they failed to really stretch into the role as he wanted them to.

He has known for a while now. It is time to try something new, to work a scene with somebody stronger. Somebody unlike the rabbits, with more depth, range, and power.

Somebody like the son. Yes, that one would be different, not a rabbit at all.

They were too easy, the rabbits he followed home. So unsuspecting. He can almost read their minds. But you can't be doing this, not to me.

And they would all realize at the same time, as he did something so interesting, so completely shattering to their little rabbit minds, that he did mean them. It was happening to them.

That's his favorite moment, that moment of realization.

He takes a long sip of his drink, letting the ice cube clink against his front teeth.

It is like Shakespeare, he thinks. That great, tragic moment of self-awareness. All the great works of theater have that. His are just a little more immediate, that's all.

He finishes his drink and raises a finger for another.

In a few hours it will be evening. Perhaps tonight would be a good time to mingle with the rabbits.

CHAPTER 23

R.J. snapped awake in his office chair with the telephone ringing.

Somehow he had let himself doze off as he sat there. He'd been having a dream that his mother caught him in a hot tub with Casey. Belle opened her mouth to scold him and the water turned red.

He shivered and rubbed his eyes, glad the phone had ended the dream. He wasn't sure he wanted to know how it would have turned out.

Wanda stuck her head in the door.

"Phone call for Rip van Winkle," she said. "It's a Detective Bertelli?"

"Thanks, Wanda," R.J. said and picked up the receiver. "Angelo," he said. "What's up?"

"I had this idea," Bertelli said. "Maybe it flies, maybe it doesn't. But I was thinking about those tapes that got stolen. And I thought, if only we could of seen 'em, we could of made a composite with all the disguises and have a picture of the killer."

"I know that, Angelo. I'm sorry."

"So then I says, Hey! Youse guys have seen the tapes! You and Miss Wingate! It's practically the same as if you saw him live, right? So let's pull out the old Identi-Kit and make a composite from memory!"

R.J. laughed. "You thought of that by yourself, huh?"

"Yeah, you know. The lieutenant is kind of following the book here—"

"That's not exactly a surprise," R.J. said.

Bertelli ignored the interruption. "And technically, you're not witnesses, on account of you seen a tape of an alleged suspect who we can't really pin to nothing, and not the crime. So this ain't strictly procedure, but since we got jack shit at the moment, I figured, what the fuck. So what do you think?"

"I think I'll vote for you in the next election for lieutenant," R.J. said. "It's a great idea, Angelo. When do you want us?"

"The thing is, I gotta run it by Kates."

"Oh, boy."

"I got to, R.J. That's policy, *capish?* So hows about youse guys meet me at his office in ninety minutes?"

"He's not gonna go for it, Angelo."

"Hey, you never know."

"I know this: You put my name on anything, I don't care if it's Toys for Tots, and he won't like it."

"I gotta do it this way, R.J. That's the rules. I'm sorry."

"All right, Angelo. Ninety minutes."

R.J. hung up, sure that the idea was dead before it got off the ground. But it was a good enough idea that it was worth the try anyway. He called Casey.

It took him forty-five minutes to track her down. When he finally got to her, she was in the West Nineties, interviewing a man who had been a judge in the first beauty contest Belle had won so long ago.

She couldn't, or wouldn't, come to the phone. So R.J. went to get her.

He had loaded her, protesting, into a cab and filled her in on Angelo's scheme on the way downtown. She thought it was a pretty good idea too.

"But an artist?" she asked as the cab ground to a stop in midtown. "Don't they use a computer for that now?"

"New York's Finest are a little old-fashioned. And anyway, the individual precincts do pretty much what they want. Angelo must like the artist."

Outside the cab, on the corner of 42nd Street, a man played a wild drum solo on a manhole lid. He leaped up, arms in the air, and harangued the lightpole. He saw R.J. watching and stepped over to the cab and glared through the window.

The cab moved on. Through the back window R.J. watched the man shake his fist, then squat over the manhole lid and start drumming again.

"There's just one thing," R.J. said to Casey, turning back around again. "The politics of this thing are a little screwed up. We have to get Kates's approval."

"Lieutenant Kates? The talking ape in the green jacket? Who are we kidding, R.J.?"

"Angelo seems to think he can pull this off."

"I'll believe it when I see it."

They pulled up in front of the precinct with almost two minutes to kill before they were supposed to meet Bertelli. But by the time they'd waded through the tide pool of whores, pimps, drug dealers, rapists, beating victims, con men, three-card monte dealers, and winos and up to the second floor, where Kates's office was, they were five minutes late.

Bertelli was already into his pitch as Casey and R.J.

came in. He stopped and looked up at them.

"Thanks for coming," he said politely.

"Sit down, Brooks. Miss Wingate," Kates said in a flat voice. Boggs sneered at them from a chair by the window.

R.J. and Casey sat in two wooden chairs, and Bertelli resumed.

"It occurred to me," he said, in his best night-school accent, "that we could facilitate the investigation and at the same time achieve a certain tactical edge by utilizing what is in actuality a standard resource."

R.J., sitting on a wooden chair next to Casey, had to snicker at the lost expression on Boggs's face as Bertelli spoke. The poor dumb sap looks like he needs a translator, R.J. thought.

Boggs caught the snicker and glared at R.J.

Lieutenant Kates was shaking his head. "It's a waste of time," he sneered. "These two are scamming us, trying to scam the Department, and I don't buy it."

Bertelli shook his head. "With respect, Lieutenant, departmental policy mandates the procedure in cases—"

"Don't 'mandate' me, Angelo. I know what departmental policy is. And it also *mandates* that the officer in charge of the investigation has broad discretionary powers in determining the course of the investigation. That's me—and I'm not going to spend the time and money on helping these two make monkeys of the NYPD."

R.J. stood up. "We don't need to make a monkey of you, Fred. You're doing fine on your own. You and your Neanderthal pal here," he said with a nod at Boggs.

Boggs stood up too and faced R.J. with a mean glower on his face. "All right, Brooks," he said. His big hands curled into fists. "This is as good a time as any."

"Sit down and shut up, Boggs." Kates's voice cracked like a whip, but Boggs stared a second longer before obeying.

"Get out of here, Brooks," the lieutenant said. "Next time I see you in here, you're going to be answering formal charges. Now get lost."

R.J. deliberately turned his back on Kates. "Coming, Miss Wingate?"

She stood up and gave Kates a look, cool and distantly amused. "Absolutely, Mr. Brooks," she said.

Bertelli stood up too. He leaned over and whispered, "Wait for me at the front desk," then turned to deal with his superior officer.

R.J. gave Casey his arm. She took it and they strolled out, with Kates's voice already grating at Bertelli.

"I'm afraid Angelo is in some deep shit," he said.

"I think he's used to it," Casey said. "It can't be easy, being the only guy on the Force with a three-digit IQ."

They sat downstairs by the front door for ten minutes before Bertelli came down. He looked cool and unruffled, in spite of having just gone through a ten-minute tongue-lashing.

He straightened his cuffs as he joined them. "Sorry about that, guys," he said. "But I have to follow procedure."

"I still think it was a good idea, Angelo," R.J. said. "It would have helped a lot."

"I think so too," Bertelli said. "But the lieutenant doesn't agree, and he's the boss. He's given me a direct order to drop the whole idea."

"So what do we do now?" Casey asked.

Bertelli winked. "Disobey orders," he said.

"Thataboy," said Casey.

"Let's get back downtown onto my turf. I got a police artist stashed there who can do this for us, and Kates will be none the wiser."

"That last part goes without saying," R.J. said.

The police artist was a guy of about forty-five, with thinning reddish hair and a drooping red mustache.

He hardly looked at them at all. Instead he stared at his sketch pad through glasses with lenses like Coke bottles as they described the killer in his various disguises.

"What we'd like," Bertelli told the artist, "is some kind of idea of how the guy looks without the disguises. You know, kind of average appearance?"

The artist shrugged. "Let's have it," he said.

Bertelli motioned to R.J., who sat down and closed his eyes, concentrating as hard as he could on the details of the three faces. R.J. gave him the priest first, then the drunk, then the newsman.

When he was done, Casey took the chair nearest the artist and went through the same three descriptions. She also added her brief memory of the Pakistani cab driver.

" 'Kay," the artist said when Casey was done. "Gimme a minute."

It was actually six minutes later when he stubbed out his cigarette and shoved a sheet of paper into Bertelli's hands before disappearing down the hallway.

Bertelli looked it over, raised an eyebrow, and handed it to R.J. "What do you think?"

R.J. took the paper and glanced down at it. The bland face that looked up at him could have been anybody. But if you half squinted, you could see that face as all the others.

R.J. nodded and passed the picture to Casey.

"It looks good, Angelo," he said.

Bertelli looked insulted. "Course it looks good. What'd you expect?"

Casey looked up from the sketch. "So what do we do with it?"

"Well," said Bertelli with a shrug, "things being what they are with the lieutenant, there's not a whole lot I can do officially. In fact, I was kinda hoping you might do something with it, R.J."

Casey looked at R.J. and raised an eyebrow.

"I got just the thing," R.J. said.

CHAPTER 24

Outside the precinct R.J. flagged a cab. As it pulled to the curb, a bald man in a three-piece suit shoved at Casey with an expensive briefcase and grabbed for the door handle.

R.J. yanked him back by the collar and the belt and walked him into a lightpost.

"Hey, what the fuck—" the bald guy started to say. *BONG*. R.J. rang his forehead off the post.

"Sorry," R.J. said. "This cab is taken."

"You're in a lot of trouble, asshole. I'm a lawyer."

"Then it sounds like *you're* the one in trouble," R.J. said. The guy thought he was going to say more, but when R.J. took half a step toward him he shut up.

R.J. turned and, stepping to the cab, opened the door for Casey, who glared at him before getting in.

R.J. heard steps behind him and turned. The lawyer, briefcase raised, was rushing at him. But at the last minute he rushed right past, pretending he was just hailing another cab.

Grinning, R.J. got in.

"We could have gotten another cab easily enough, R.J."

He turned to Casey. She still looked miffed.

He shrugged. "So could he. In fact, he did."

"I can take care of myself, you know. And I don't like the idea of having you running around like a cheap thug defending my honor."

"Listen, I'm a very expensive thug."

"At least stop looking so pleased with yourself, like you just did something noble."

R.J. gave her his best sour face and turned to look out the window.

I don't get it, he thought. If I did nothing I'd be a spineless, gutless weeny. So I run the guy off and I'm a thug. He sighed and wished he could figure this woman out.

"Where are you taking me?" she said after several minutes of silence.

She wasn't sulking anymore. She looked composed, cool, completely neutral, and that bothered him just as much: that she could shake it off so fast, like whatever he did was not really that important to her.

Get a grip, he told himself.

"We're going to see a friend of mine," he said, holding up the brown envelope Bertelli had given them. It contained twenty photocopies of the sketch.

She arched an eyebrow. "You have friends?"

"Just a couple."

"And what does this one do? Break legs for a bookie?"

R.J. grinned. "That's my *other* friend. This guy is in urban intelligence."

"Say what?"

"Hookshot is a little hard to explain," he told her.

She shook her head. "I'll bet."

"I'm giving him the composite, see what he can do with it."

"We're counting on a guy named Hookshot?"

"That's right."

She looked away. "Just don't ask me to team up with anybody named Tinkerbell."

Casey was not impressed with Hookshot's office, either. The midtown news kiosk was shabby and festooned with cheesy tabloids. It looked its age.

"Oh, brother," Casey muttered as they got out of the cab. "I've never seen a newsstand that beat up."

"Relax, will you?" R.J. told her.

"It looks like a Bowery Boys set."

They walked around to the front of the kiosk. A middle-aged man in a gray coat hurried past. At the last moment he snaked out a hand and grabbed for a *Times*.

From inside the booth there was a streak of silver, so fast it was only a bright blur. The gray-coated man jerked to a halt.

His coat sleeve was pinned to the counter by a steel hook.

On the other end of the hook was Hookshot.

He flashed his teeth at the man. "Fifty cents, please," Hookshot said.

"Jesus Christ," said the man and Casey at the same time.

The man fished out the change as R.J. laughed.

"*Hook*-shot?" Casey said.

"You got it."

"Jesus Christ," she repeated as the gray-coated man scuttled away.

"Nice snag," R.J. told his friend.

Hookshot gave Casey the once-over. "You too, R.J."

"This is Casey Wingate, Hookshot."

"The TV producer?"

R.J. nodded. "That's right.

Hookshot looked doubtful. "Weeelll, if R.J. says you're okay . . ."

"I do say."

Hookshot held out his hand. "Nice to meet you."

Casey took his hand and shook it. "It's mutual, I'm sure."

"I got something for you," R.J. told him, flipping the envelope onto the counter.

"This have to do with your mama?"

"That's right. I need your help."

Hookshot opened the envelope. "You got it." He pulled out the picture and studied it for a minute.

"He looks like a shoe salesman," Hookshot said, studying the picture. "You sure that's him?"

"That's him," R.J. said, wishing he felt that much confidence.

"Uh-huh. You want me to check all the Thom McAn's in Manhattan? 'Cause I look at this face, and it ain't a Florsheim's face, know what I mean?"

"I know."

"Maybe I oughta take a shoehorn along."

"All right, Hookshot. I got twenty copies in there. Pass 'em out to your best boys."

Hookshot shook his head. "I told you we don't use that word, R.J. They the minimensch."

"I don't care what you call 'em. Just find this guy, all right?"

Hookshot smiled. "If he's out there, we'll find him."

*It is dark now. He's finished three or four drinks. The greasy
sandwich he ate as he sat at the bar lies in his stomach like a lead
weight, but that doesn't matter.*

It is time.

*He feels the thing inside him uncoil and stretch in preparation
for what he will do tonight.*

*He stands up and stretches too. The clock over the bar says it's
ten after seven. That gives him twenty minutes to get across town;
plenty of time.*

*He settles his bar tab and leaves a tip. The bartender tells him
thank you without really seeing him, just like everyone else never
saw him, but that's all right. He'll be seen later tonight, he is sure
of that.*

━━━━━━━━━━━●━━━━━━━━━━━

Frank had been coming to the meetings here in St.
Mark's for twenty-two years. He had been leading the
meetings off and on for the last eight. Although the position of secretary was supposed to rotate, somehow it
kept coming back to Frank, and so he stood in front of
them tonight and scanned the faces as he had so many
times.

There were two new faces tonight: a woman who
had clearly come with Allison C., and a plain-looking
man sitting by himself in the back row.

Frank nodded and cleared his throat. "My name is
Frank. I'm an alcoholic."

"Hi, Frank," the others chorused back to him.

After the standard opening of the greeting and a few
quick announcements, Frank went back to his chair
and the meeting began.

A large man named Ben stood up. He was almost a
caricature of a big drinker, with his red nose and big
belly. He was sweating heavily, although the evening
was cool. Frank recognized the signs: Ben was wres-
tling with an almost overwhelming need for a drink.

Talking about it would help. So Ben talked.

He talked about having a drink with the boys, how it had helped him know who he was, and how it had slowly turned into lots of drinks with the boys, and finally into drinking with or without boys, girls or dogs. Until his life was a series of drinks, nothing more.

When he was done, Allison's friend introduced herself. Her name was Susan and she had a story to tell too. It was a familiar one: She'd started drinking just a little to ease the pressure of job and family expectations. The drinks steadied her, gave her confidence. She believed the family and co-workers really liked her more when she drank. So she drank more.

Soon the downward spiral began: lost jobs, loved ones pulling away, her life crumbling around her, her health deteriorating. And now she had almost nothing left to lose—except her drinking, the one friend who had stayed with her no matter how bad things got.

And now she realized it was not her friend at all and she didn't know what she was going to do.

There was a short pause when Susan sat down again. Then the other newcomer got to his feet.

For a moment he just stood in the back of the room. Then he moved slowly up the aisle to the front.

He turned and faced the meeting, an ordinary-looking man—and yet, thought Frank, there was something about his eyes. They were gray and gleamed coldly.

"My name is John," he said softly, "I'm an alcoholic."

"Hi, John," the others said.

"I am—an ordinary man," he said, looking around the room at them. "My face is standard issue—I could be anybody. When you see me on the street, you don't give me a second glance, not ever. Even my name is ordinary: John. Everything about me is so completely plain that you would never guess there is a war going on inside me twenty-four hours a day.

"I'm a drunk."

He paused here and swept his chilly eyes across the group. Frank felt a small shiver as the eyes passed over him, but he could not say why.

"As long as I can remember, I have been plain. Average. Ordinary. Banal. Common. Prosaic. Routine, dry, dull, colorless, drab, lackluster, monotonous, tedious, uninteresting, everyday, unexceptional, mundane. Ordinary."

His voice rose through the last sentence, and when he paused it was so quiet Frank thought he could hear a mouse moving through the church upstairs and he realized he was holding his breath.

"Ordinary," John resumed quietly. "Except when I drink. When I drink I feel special." He slammed his hands together and Frank nearly jumped out of his seat.

"Drinking makes me *special*. I know that has happened to you too, or you wouldn't be here. You like to feel special; we all do. We're all human. The same things are inside all of us." There was a strange gleam in his gray eyes as he said that, and once again Frank shivered.

But John had them all in the palm of his hand, and Frank thought he had never seen anything like it, not in all his twenty-two years of coming to AA meetings. Sometimes there were meetings that degenerated into can-you-top-this sessions as each speaker tried to go one better than the speaker before. But this topped them all. This John was a real spellbinder.

His story was not so different. It could have been the story of almost anyone here. But the way he told it . . .

Frank felt gooseflesh forming up and down his back

as John told of drinking a fifth of vodka a day before his fifteenth birthday. Something about the story seemed like a performance, and that was a little unnerving. But it was so compelling, Frank eventually let go and just listened, swept away like everyone else in the room.

———————————◆———————————

Look at them eat it up. So gullible. So weak.

Rabbits.

They deserve to die, all of them. Huddling miserably together to trade their pitiful stories of puking and humiliation.

And he feels the slow uncoiling inside him, the wonderful thing stirring, waking, becoming fully ready for what lies ahead.

This is, after all, just a warmup, a curtain raiser. The featured entertainment will begin soon after.

Very soon now.

CHAPTER 25

I still think we ought to send the picture to the local news," Casey said. "Let them put it on the air."

R.J., bent over to unlock his door, looked up at her. "You can't really believe that," he said as he pushed the door open.

"I know you don't like TV people, R.J., but you shouldn't let a prejudice stand in the way of doing something right."

R.J. snorted as she followed him in. "If I don't like cats, that's a prejudice. If I don't like piranhas, that's common sense."

Something hit him hard between the shoulder blades. He turned to see that it was Casey's shoulder bag. It was heavy. It hurt.

"I am not a piranha," she said. "Buster, you had better respect what I do or I'll teach you the hard way."

"I wasn't talking about you," R.J. protested. "I just meant—"

"What is it you think I do for a living, R.J.?"

"I know what you do. I'm sorry about the piranha remark."

"Because you have been making cracks about this just about nonstop, and I've had it up to here."

"All right, all right, for Christ's sake, I said I'm sorry." R.J. held up both hands.

She snorted at him and spun away toward the bedroom.

R.J. followed.

"Casey. Would you hold it for a second?"

She kept going into the bedroom.

"Casey." He leaned forward and put a hand on her shoulder. She pulled away but turned to face him.

"Listen," he said, "we're going to be cooped up together for a couple more days. Don't be so touchy, okay?"

She arched an eyebrow. "Was I being touchy?"

"Yeah, you were."

"Oh. I'm sorry if I overreacted. But you're *not* touchy, are you?"

"Look—"

"So I guess if I made remarks about your profession, you wouldn't mind, isn't that right?"

"Casey—"

"Because I think that taking pictures of other people screwing without their knowledge, for money, must be about the vilest, sleaziest, scummiest, rottenest thing in the world, and I would think that the kind of brainless, heartless, soulless, amoral orangutan who does that sort of work would be the last one to make remarks about what *normal* people do for a living, wouldn't you agree, R.J.?"

And she turned away, leaving him with his mouth hanging open.

The next day was one of the hardest R.J. could remember.

The tension between him and Casey had gotten worse. They ate a miserable, cold dinner with no more than ten words between them. The high point of the meal came when he passed her the salt and she said "Thank you."

And yet, that night, he had figured he was in the dog house and went to sleep on the couch. In the middle of the night he opened one eye, aware that he was no longer alone.

She stood there in the harsh light from the window, looking down at him. She did not say a word. He wasn't sleeping, exactly, but he figured he must be dreaming. The look on her face was soft, inward. Her expression was like that found in one of those Renaissance religious pictures of the Madonna.

Then she raised both arms over her head and slipped off her nightgown. She stood there naked. The hollows of her body glimmered. Neither of them spoke.

She slid down onto him, stretching out on top of him on the couch.

For a moment she just lay there. R.J. could feel the warmth of her body against his. His pulse pounded, jump-started from sleep to top speed in one heartbeat. He reached a hand up and cupped her butt. He dug his other hand under the weight of her hair and rested it on the back of her neck. He felt her sigh heavily against his neck, and then she lay her mouth on his.

Once again they made love, gently this time. When they were done she got up, still without a word, and went back into the bedroom.

In the morning he couldn't be sure it had happened.

She was cool and distant as they got ready for the day, eating her plain yogurt and fresh fruit.

R.J. had always had trouble focusing until after his coffee. He slurped it fast, wanting to say something, anything, to get her to talk, to help him figure out what the hell was going on. But by the time he had cleared his head and was ready to speak with her, she was gone.

R.J. finished his high-cholesterol breakfast of bacon and eggs, had a final cup of coffee, and went to the office.

Wanda was already there when he arrived.

"Morning, Boss," she said cheerfully.

"Good morning," R.J. said, but his heart wasn't really in it. "Any messages?"

"Mrs. Burkette called," she said, trying to hide her feline amusement.

"Oh? What did she say?"

"You don't want to know," Wanda said.

"Uh-huh. Fine. Nothing else?"

"That's it."

R.J. went on into his inner office and closed the door. He stuck a cigar in his mouth, leaned back in the chair, and tried to persuade himself that he was working. He didn't have any luck.

What the hell am I doing? he wondered. My mother's killer is out there and all I can do is sit in this goddamned overstuffed chair.

He tried to believe that he was doing all he could. He ran over the list: Uncle Hank was polishing up the profile down in Quantico, Arthur was digging around in Hollywood, and Hookshot's army was circulating, armed with the composite picture. There was no other lead to exploit, no other opening—but he felt he should be doing something more than leaning back in his chair and thinking about Casey.

The only problem was that he couldn't think of anything worth doing.

So R.J. sat in his chair for three-quarters of an hour. At the end of that time he'd had enough and stalked out the door.

"I'll see you later," he told Wanda.

"Bye, boss," she called after him, flinching as he slammed the door.

It was raining again. It seemed like it had been raining a lot lately, like every time he stepped outside. He knew that wasn't true, but that's what it felt like.

He dropped his soggy cigar in the gutter and started walking anyway. Maybe walking in the rain would work as a kind of penance, help him put his life back on track through suffering. Maybe it would help clear his head, give him perspective.

On the other hand, maybe he'd just get soaking wet and catch pneumonia.

The rain let up after ten blocks, settling into a light drizzle. Still, by the time he got to his mother's apartment he was wet to the skin.

He hadn't started out to walk to the apartment, but that's where his feet had taken him, and he didn't argue.

Tony held the door open. "Hey, Mr. Brooks. You're wet."

R.J. stepped into the lobby. "Yeah, Tony, I know. That happens to you when you don't have enough sense to come in out of the rain."

Tony shook a finger at him. "You get outta those wet clothes, Mr. Brooks. You'll get sick or somethin'."

"Yeah, I will. Thanks, Tony."

On the elevator up to the apartment, R.J. wondered

again what he was doing here. He hadn't come just to
have a quiet place to sit and think. He was too antsy for
that.

As he unlocked the door he knew he was heading for
his mother's journals again. And it occurred to him
that even though he was pretty sure they did not hold
the key to his mother's murder, in some way he felt certain they held the key to solving the turbulence that was
slamming through him, keeping him so far off-center.
By solving his mother, he might solve himself, and even
Casey. It didn't make sense, but he believed it.

In her office he sat in the chair with a stack of the
journals within easy reach.

He reached for the volume on the top of the small
pile. It was from eight years ago. He remembered the
period well enough. His mother had made a whole series of "business trips" to New York. It had seemed like
he was having to dodge her every other week.

And somehow she would track him down, run into
him on the street, and force him into accepting her invitations: to parties with her fruity friends, to the tacky,
effete Broadway musicals she seemed to like, and to the
awful, cloying Tea Room.

He had been busy that year, and yet he had to put
things on hold to trot after his mother, and he had re-
sented it. She kept pulling him along, and he kept trying to get away—trying gracefully at first and, as the
year wore on, trying any way he could, often rudely.

All in all it had not been the most successful year in
their relationship.

He opened the book and began to read.

> I feel desperately unhappy about R.J. No matter
> what I try he keeps pushing me away. I can't say
> that I blame him; I have always been a rotten
> mother, and now I suppose it's coming home to

roost. Still, it's tearing into me like some horrible carrion-eating bird.

I see him closing himself off from so much of the world—from practically everything except his work, which God knows is not very elevating, and I know he will pay for that later in his life. I shudder when I think how tiny and pointless my life would have been if it were not for the accidental exposure I've had to some of the arts. And now R.J. is halfway gone down the same road.

And he won't let me near him! I'm so frustrated I could scream. I feel like this is the greatest failure of my life—my own, my only son, and he can't really stand to be in the same room with me. I can see that in his eyes when I manage to "run into" him—after hours of stalking and planning!

He can't wait to get away, to be anywhere but with me, and worst of all, I know it's all my own fault.

R.J. let the book drop into his lap.

It wasn't all her fault. Sure, she'd been an indifferent mother when he was a kid. She'd had a career, and she'd thought that was more important than hanging around the house and playing catch with her kid.

A kid who was so self-centered he thought having Mom around whenever he wanted her was the most important thing in the world; and because she was out making a living instead, that made her a rotten person.

What a jerk he was. He was still acting like that kid, couldn't let go of a kid's stubborn sense that he was the center of the universe and nothing mattered more than what he wanted.

That was why he had pushed her away: because he had never grown up enough to admit that she had a life outside of his, so he had to punish her. Play by my rules or I'll take my ball, kick down the playground, and go home.

He had made his mother miserable because he couldn't grow up, let go of her mistakes—and his own—and let her be herself with him.

And what a strong, patient person she was! She wouldn't give up, like anybody else would have—like he would have, for certain. She kept trying, right up to the very end. Trying to get him to wake up, to see her for what she was, to grow up, to let go of all the mean-spirited, small-minded bitterness he had made his life out of.

She would reach out, he would push her hand away.

She would try again, he would push her away again.

He couldn't open up to her and couldn't understand that she was trying to open up to him.

And now the same thing was happening with Casey.

R.J. hadn't cried since he was a kid, and he wasn't about to start now.

But he sure wished he could.

CHAPTER 26

It was full dark when R.J. left the apartment.

What he had read, and what he thought about what he had read, had battered him.

He thought about his mother, dead before he could really know her. He thought about his life, and what a total fucking mess he'd made of it.

And he thought about Casey. She was right to think he was a—what had she called him?—a "brainless, amoral orangutan." Well, he was that.

He'd walled off everything inside himself and slid into a dirty business because he had to keep himself from feeling anything or he couldn't even do his job.

And now he was feeling things, and it was tearing him up, because he didn't know how to do it. And because of that, when he needed more than ever before just to do his job, to find his mother's killer, he was screwing that up too.

R.J. started walking. He had no idea where he was

going. He supposed he should check with Casey, to make sure she was all right. After all, he was supposed to be guarding her.

But he wasn't sure he could face her without bursting into tears and making a complete jerk of himself. So he just let his feet call the shots and wandered downtown along the edge of Central Park.

He was so busy with the turmoil inside his head that he wasn't paying attention to where he was going. And so when the man spoke to him, he snapped alert with astonishment.

"Can I help you?" the man said politely.

The guy was wearing a bow tie and a white apron.

R.J. looked around him, totally floored. He was in a bar.

Somehow he'd walked into the place without realizing where he was and bellied right up to the bar, still oblivious.

But his feet were giving him a message. He wanted a drink. He looked at his hands and saw they were shaking just a little.

He looked past the bartender to the cool, clean line of bottles, like a platoon of crack soldiers standing at attention on the parade ground.

His mouth was watering. His head was buzzing, and he could feel all the cells in his body calling out to the gleaming parade of bottles.

He wanted a drink.

Oh, God, how he wanted a drink.

"Hey, you want a drink, or what?" the bartender said, tapping one hand on the bar.

R.J. took a deep breath. His head whirled.

"Yes. I want a drink," he said and swallowed.

The bartender nodded.

"What'll it be?"

"Nothing." R.J. turned and walked on unsteady legs

for the door. He could hear the bartender mutter, "Well, fuck you." But he made it out the door anyway, without screaming, without collapsing into a puddle on the floor, without diving back toward the bar and begging for a shot of oblivion.

On the sidewalk he stood still for a few minutes, just breathing. The air was cold and felt half clean, as if rain was coming behind the breeze.

He'd almost started drinking again. Not that he couldn't handle it. He'd always handled it before.

But this time felt different. Could he really handle it this time, the same as he'd done in the past, if he had a few? R.J. didn't know the answer to that, but he didn't feel like pushing his luck. He suspected the answer was no.

When he had stopped shaking and no longer felt dizzy, R.J. turned his steps crosstown. He was hungry as hell by the time he got back to his apartment.

"Where have you been?" Casey greeted him. "Your dinner's cold."

"I'll eat it anyway," R.J. said. "What is it?"

"Meat," she said.

He sat at the table in the kitchen and wolfed down a small steak, a stone-cold potato, and a salad with a lot of strange things in it.

"Jicama," Casey said, leaning in the doorway and watching him pull out a strip of some weird, crunchy vegetable.

"What's that?"

"Just eat it, it's good."

He ate it. It was good—crisp, clean, and sweet-tasting. He ate all of it, and every scrap of steak, including the fat, and the cold potato. He was surprised at how hungry he was.

When he was done he got up to make coffee. Casey was still leaning in the doorway.

"That was very good," he told her. "Thanks."

"Your friend Hookshot called," she said.

He stopped dead. "He *called*? Hookshot called? On the telephone?"

"Is that unusual?"

"Yes. Hookshot hates telephones. He never uses them if he can avoid it."

Casey shook her head. "You have odd friends."

"When did he call? What did he say?"

"He's got something for you. He wouldn't say what."

"He's found something," R.J. said. "Something to do with the killer. He wouldn't use the phone if it wasn't important."

He could feel the adrenaline throbbing through him. It gave him a half-sick edge. He wanted to hit somebody, and the meal that had been sitting so pleasantly in his stomach a minute before felt like it had turned to lead. He hurried for the door, grabbing at a coat.

"Hey," said Casey. "Why don't you just call him?"

"He won't answer. I told you, Hookshot hates telephones."

He made it to midtown in fifteen minutes. Hookshot called out from behind his screen of hanging papers and magazines. "Damn, R.J., where you *been*?"

"I came as soon as I heard, Hookshot. What've you got?"

Hookshot shook his head. "Make me use the goddamned TEL-o-phone, man, and you know I hate that shit."

"I'm sorry, all right?"

Hookshot leaned out to his left. A twelve-year-old kid was sitting on a skateboard with his back to the kiosk. He wore baggy sweats and a helmet.

"Benny!" Hookshot yelled, and the kid looked up. "Yeah?"

"Get your raggedy ass over here, man."

Benny stood up, clutching his skateboard with one hand and pulling at the seat of his pants with the other.

"I'm here, all right?"

Hookshot nodded at R.J. "Tell this dude what you saw."

"What for?"

Hookshot sighed and raised an eyebrow at R.J.

"Yeah, I get it," R.J. said, and he pulled out a five-dollar bill. He smoothed it so the kid could see it. "What'd you see, kid?"

Benny eyed the fiver, then looked at Hookshot, who shrugged. Benny shrugged and turned back to R.J. with an expression of pathetic patience.

"You know St. Mark's?"

"The church?"

Benny stared at R.J. with disbelief. "No, the synagogue. Course it's a fucking church."

Hookshot leaned out and cuffed Benny—not hard, but the kid got the message.

"All right, shit, so St. Mark's the church, okay?"

"Okay. What about it?"

Benny shrugged. "So I'm going by there—this is last night you unnerstan. It's like nine o'clock. And I see the guy coming out, okay?"

He held out his hand for the five-dollar bill. R.J. pulled it away. "Not so fast, kid. You saw *what* guy?"

Benny sighed again and gave him the look that asked, Who is this dope? "The guy in the picture, who'd you think, it was Donald Fucking Trump?"

R.J. looked at Hookshot. "Does he mean the composite picture?"

"That's right."

R.J. turned back to the kid. "Are you sure it was him?"

Sigh. "Course I'm sure. What, I look stupid?"

"Benny's a wiseass," Hookshot said. "But if he says he saw him, you best believe he saw him."

R.J. put the five-dollar bill back in his pocket.

"Hey!" said Benny.

But R.J. pulled his hand out again, this time with a ten-dollar bill.

"More like it," said Benny.

CHAPTER 27

St. Mark's was one of the few old East Side churches that hadn't been torn down to make room for high-rise co-ops. It looked squat, old and dirty, but it had a steeple and all the other working parts.

It also had a small rectory attached on the back side. There was a light on in the window when R.J. got there, so he knocked on the door with a clear conscience.

After a couple of moments the door swung wide and R.J., wearing a meek face so he wouldn't scare any church mice, suddenly found himself looking straight up.

"Can I help you?" boomed the man. He was at least 6'5" and looked like he'd been lifting weights most of his life.

"Jesus," said R.J. without thinking.

"No, but I can take a message. What can I do for you?"

"Uh . . ." began R.J. "I'm looking for the, uh, preacher here?"

"That's me," the man bellowed. "Come on in." He stepped aside and R.J. stumbled in.

R.J. followed into a study lined with books. He caught a couple of titles, like *The Living Bible* and *Historical Jesus*. The giant stepped around behind a massive wooden desk and sat in a swivel chair. The chair groaned.

"Sit down. I'm Jim Mudge," he said. "How can I help you?"

R.J. collected his wits.

"My name is R.J. Brooks," he began, reaching one of his business cards across the desk to Reverend Mudge.

"I know who you are," Mudge said. "I've seen you on the evening news lately." But he took the card anyway.

"Well, then I can cut to the chase. I have reason to believe that my mother's killer was here at the church last night."

Reverend Mudge nodded but didn't say anything.

"He was seen leaving the church around nine o'clock. I wonder if you can tell me what he might have been doing here."

Mudge leaned back in his chair and laced his hands behind his neck. The fabric of his shirt strained and looked like it might shred. "I know exactly what he was doing here last night," Mudge said. "But beyond that I can't help you."

R.J. shook his head. "I don't get it."

"Last night was the weekly meeting of Alcoholics Anonymous," Mudge said. "Do you know anything about how AA works?"

"Yeah, I do."

"Well then you know that the whole program depends on anonymity. I can't give you any names at all."

"But you're in charge of the church here, you must know the guy that runs the meetings."

He nodded. "That's right. But I can't tell you his name."

"Why not?"

"That would violate the confidentiality of the meetings."

"That's understandable, but—"

Mudge cut him off. "And even if I were to talk to the guy who leads the meetings, I don't think he's likely to give you much more."

"Reverend—we're talking about murder here."

Mudge nodded. "I understand that."

"I don't think you do. This guy is a serial killer. He's killed at least a dozen people and he's going to kill more if I don't stop him. These are not clean hits, Reverend. This is a sick guy. He tortures them. He dresses things up to look pretty. And when he's done it's so pretty that hard-core cops who think they've seen it all are chucking their lunch all over the floor."

"Mr. Brooks—"

"This is the guy who killed my mother, Reverend. And he's going to kill again, that's a fact. He's out there laughing at me, and laughing at the cops, and laughing at you for protecting him, and I would knock down Mother Teresa, run over Albert Schweitzer, and shoot the Pope to get at this guy. Do you understand me now?"

When R.J. was finished he was surprised to find that he was on his feet, knuckles on the big desk, and leaning in only inches from Mudge's face.

R.J. took a deep breath and straightened.

"Sorry, padre," he said and sat down again.

Mudge was chewing on his lip and breathing a little

harder. "I'll call Frank," he said and reached for the telephone.

R.J. leaned back in his chair and concentrated on breathing for a minute. Jesus, he thought. I sort of came unglued there. But hell, if it works . . .

"Hello, Frank? Jim Mudge . . . Fine, listen, I've got a small problem for you, do you have a minute?"

———————◆———————

The deli was on the corner of 3rd and Lex. It had been there as long as R.J. remembered, and probably a lot longer.

When R.J. walked in forty minutes later, Frank was waiting for him in a booth at the back of the room, directly across from a display case stuffed with pastrami.

Frank was a wiry guy in his sixties with thin gray hair he kept slick and a set of little cheater glasses on his nose. He had that look of quiet strength, the strength of endurance, that R.J. had come to associate with long-time AA members.

They shook hands and R.J. slid into the booth opposite Frank. When he was settled, he saw that Frank had been sizing him up in his mild way.

"How long have you been sober, R.J.?" Frank asked.

R.J. was startled. "Jesus, it shows?"

Frank smiled and gave his head a half shake. "Only to me. I've been doing this for a long time now. I just see little things that add up, and I take a guess. Just a guess, but I'm usually right."

"Uh-huh. I'd be more interested in what you might have guessed about a guy who was at your meeting last night."

R.J. slid out one of the photocopies of the composite picture. But before he could hand it across the table Frank held up a hand.

"I'm not sure I can do that," he said. "We have pretty strict rules. We have to. That's the only way this thing can work, Mr. Brooks, and it has worked for seventy years now."

"I can appreciate that. My mother only got to work for a little more than sixty years, Frank. Then she was murdered by this guy here." He held up the picture. "Was he at your meeting last night?"

Frank studied R.J., refusing to look at the picture. "Have you been to an AA meeting, R.J.?"

"I sat in on a couple."

"Then you know that even if I wanted to—and I don't want to—I couldn't tell you anybody's name."

"Sure, I know. Bill W. Frank S. Psycho Killer P. I don't give a shit about any of that, Frank. All I want is to know if this guy was at the meeting and if you think he'll be back. And if you won't tell me, I guess I'll just go across the street to Kelley's and have a drink."

Frank looked at him for a moment longer. Then he smiled. "All right, R.J. You don't have to threaten me." He shifted his eyes to the picture and frowned. "Oh," he said. And then he clammed up.

R.J. almost jumped over the table at him. "You know him?"

Frank shrugged. "I don't know him. He was at the meeting last night, first time. I'm pretty sure it was him. He didn't look exactly like this picture here, but pretty close. I think it was him. He gave quite a speech."

"Will he be back?"

"I don't know. I never know. We always close with that, you know, asking everyone to come back. But this guy? Who knows. I don't think he was from around here."

"Why do you say that?"

"Well, I haven't seen him before. And the way he spoke—"

"What do you mean?"

Frank gave R.J. another half smile. "It's another little thing I do. I listen to people talk for a couple of minutes and I can generally guess where they came from. The region, in some cases the city."

"So where was this guy from?"

Frank shook his head. "Hard to say. Not New York, probably."

" 'Probably'? This is some hobby, Frank. The best you can do is 'not New York, probably'?"

Frank nodded. "I know. But certain people have worked at their speech, tried to make it neutral. Sometimes to get rid of an accent or a speech impediment. A lot of theater actors sound like this guy. The ones with training, you know. From the good drama schools."

R.J. leaned back in his seat. There it was again, the theater business. He felt a vein throb in his temple.

This was the guy. He was sure of it.

"Frank," he said, tapping the picture, "I think he might come back. He likes to show off, and if he thinks he's fooling you he'll do it again, rub your nose in it."

"I can't stop him from coming back, R.J. I won't."

"I'm not asking you to. I'm just letting you know, if he does come back, I'm going to be there waiting for him."

Frank looked troubled. "I'm not sure I approve of that. I'm sorry—I wish I could help you, but . . ."

"You want to help me, just forget you ever saw me and run your meetings. I'll be there."

"I don't know about that, R.J. You being there, I mean."

R.J. laughed and stood up. "You can't stop me, Frank. Remember? My name is R.J. I'm an alcoholic."

CHAPTER 28

It wasn't much of a victory. Frank was a decent guy, trying to do the right thing. Still, it was about the only win R.J. had had lately, and he felt his blood moving faster.

R.J. was getting the smell of the killer. Casey was right that he was an actor; he was sure of it now. R.J. felt closer to finding him than he had before, and the feeling was a good one.

In fact, R.J. felt so good he decided to take the subway home. The train was only about half full at this hour. But as they rattled uptown a large black man in a beret stormed into the car.

"Hey!" he shouted. Nobody looked at him.

"You people are lucky! You riding *my train!* Ain't nobody fuck with you on my train! I got a black belt in Tie-crown-doo! Y'all are *safe* now!" And then he took off his beret and moved down the train, shoving the greasy cap under the nose of every single passenger.

Most of them fumbled some change into the hat. When he came to R.J., he paused. R.J. looked up at him, smiling.

"You a transit cop?" the man asked.

"No," R.J. said.

"Then why you looking at me like that, man?"

"I'm a masochist. I was hoping to get robbed and beaten, and you just spoiled my whole day."

"Shit," the man said as he moved away. "I hate this goddamn city."

As R.J. walked the last three blocks from the train he felt his glow wearing off. So he was closer. Big deal. He had been so far from finding the guy that closer was meaningless. Besides, what did he know that he hadn't known before? That the killer talked nice? So the last thing his mother had heard would have been good diction. That was a help.

He was fucking it up. She had worried about him in her journal, and she'd been right to worry. He was at a dead end in finding this killer because he was in a dead-end life: rotten past, dismal future, and not enough brains and balls to do anything about it.

If he had any smarts at all he would talk to Casey. Maybe even talk about the future with her. Let her know how he felt about her, how she was tearing him up inside. If he'd done that with his mother things would have been different. Maybe they would have gotten along. Maybe she'd still be alive.

And maybe, R.J. thought bitterly, if I flap my arms hard enough I can fly to the moon.

By the time he got back to his apartment he had ridden the mood swing all the way through the cycle and he was feeling pretty bad. As he opened the door and saw Casey he felt better briefly—a quick shot of adrenaline: She looked great, and she was waiting for him.

"What happened?" she asked. "Guy crap out on you?"

"No," he said. "Hookshot doesn't crap out. One of his kids ID'd the picture. Guy was at an AA meeting at St. Mark's last night. AA leader says it was him."

"That's great. So what's with the face?"

"What do you mean?"

"You look like a pigeon just shit on your ice-cream cone, R.J. What's the problem?"

Here was his opening. His heart gave a quick double knock of excitement. He could tell her everything, pour out his soul and let her sponge it up. Instead, he just said, "I don't know. I'm not sure it's that much of a lead."

She looked at him like she thought he might say something else, but when he didn't she just said, "Tell me about it."

He told her about it. He ran through Benny's ID of the picture, his interview with the giant priest, and the talk with Frank.

"So now what do I know? Maybe he shows up at AA again next week. That'd be nice. If he does, I nail him. But he probably won't, and if he doesn't, where am I? Nowhere again. Or nowhere still. No closer to finding him than I was two weeks ago."

"You know, R.J.," Casey said, "you're cute, but you're dumb."

"What's that mean?"

"It means he handed it to you and you're too bone-headed to pick it up and run with it. You're acting like a quitter, and you're giving up on the only really important thing you've tried in who knows how long."

"What the hell are you talking about?"

"Listen, schmuck. We got confirmation that the picture is good, right?"

"Right. So—"

"So we know what he looks like. And now we think we know something about his past. So we can follow his back trail with the picture and find out who he is. Do you think you can catch him if you know his name and what he looks like, R.J.?"

He shook off her heavy-handed sarcasm. "You're not making sense. What do we know about his past?"

"I'm not making—For the love of God, R.J., you're supposed to be the hot-shot investigator. I'm just a piranha, remember?"

"I remember. I wish you'd drop it."

"Frank told you—what did he say? That the guy had a speech pattern like he'd gone to one of the good acting schools. So if he went to one of the good acting schools—and there aren't that many—somebody will remember him."

R.J. nodded. "It's something," he admitted.

"Asshole," she said. "What do you mean, 'something,' it's brilliant. Get to work on your big-time show-biz connections and find out what schools to call. You want to tell the cops any of this?"

"No. They haven't helped me any. All Kates wants is to see my head on his lunch plate. They get nothing from me."

"Angelo might take it bad if you don't tell him."

"Angelo has to report everything to Kates. He'll understand."

She shrugged. "Your funeral. Think you can handle the phone calls, or you want me to hold your hand?"

"Lay off, Casey."

She nodded. "That's a very strong comeback, R.J."

"Why are you on my case like this?"

"Why are *you* so pathetic all of a sudden?"

R.J. felt his stomach knot. "Is that what you think?"

"Well, for Christ's sake!" she exploded. "We've

been cooped up in here for days, and if it was up to you we'd be here forever! You are nowhere at all on solving this and you're not trying to get anywhere! She was your mother, R.J., and all you're doing is moping around and grabbing some free ass!"

"I don't see you complaining about the ass-grabbing, Casey."

He knew as he spoke it was the wrong thing to say and he would have called the words back if he could, but it was too late. She gave him a look of pure disgust and contempt.

"Well then you can consider this your notice," she said. She turned and walked toward the bedroom door.

"Casey . . ." R.J. said.

She stopped and looked at him again. This look wasn't any better. "What a sleazy piece of shit you are," she said and went into the bedroom. She closed the door very firmly behind her.

———————————————●———————————————

He had been feeling it since he woke up that morning, and with the coming of full night it is so strong he is almost shaking with the power of it, the roaring in his veins and the surge through his head that is almost like singing.

"Hallelujah," he sings to himself.

"What was that?" asks the bartender from fifteen feet away.

"Nothing," he says. "Nothing at all."

The bartender nods and says nothing. Good man, that. Knows the value of silence. He drains his drink and raises a finger for another.

He can drink all day and it won't affect him. Not when he is like this. Not when he can feel that splendid thing uncoiling inside him, flexing, fangs bared, ready to strike.

It is time.

Oh yes, it is time now, time at last, time to do it. He can feel the certainty of it bubbling inside him, and he lets it perk, feeding it with his thoughts, teasing it, drawing out the feeling as long as he can.

This will be the best ever. Because it is personal, has always been personal. Unfinished business, something that has been hanging incomplete all these years and making him steadily, quietly furious; and now it is happening, the pattern is almost complete.

It is all coming together now, all the threads from so long ago, everything falling into a perfect pattern that he will weave into the greatest scene of his life.

Tomorrow. That will be the day.

He sips.

And he laughs quietly as it comes to him how he will begin.

CHAPTER 29

R.J. woke up feeling like his head was packed with sand and all his joints were fused. He was lying face-down on the couch, still dressed, where he had finally dropped, exhausted, at around four-thirty.

He noticed right away when he opened his eyes. In spite of being dead tired, in spite of feeling like he'd been beaten up again, it was the first thing he noticed.

The bedroom door was open.

Casey was gone.

It must have been the sound of her leaving that woke him. He sat up. Through the open door he saw how neatly the bed was made. With a sick lurch in his stomach he stepped into the room and looked around.

There was no trace of her left behind. All her small items of makeup were gone, her toothbrush taken from the bathroom. Her clothes too, which he had watched her buy, and seen spread out across the bed and the chair. All the skirts and blouses and underwear. All gone.

Casey was gone.

She would rather take her chances with a psychotic killer than put up with him any longer.

He sank onto the bed, rubbing his eyes. It wasn't just a fight, it was the end. She wasn't coming back.

And why should she? Come back to what?

Come back to a guy who could barely function emotionally? To somebody so closed off he had never even told his own mother what he felt about her, let alone ever telling a lover anything. He had told Casey nothing at all, except that he didn't hear her objecting to the ass-grabbing.

That was great stuff, man. Real smooth-talking. Amazing that she hadn't thrown herself at his feet when she heard it.

She was right. He really was a sleazy shit. A sleazy, amoral, orangutan shit.

He flopped onto the bed and lay there for a while, unable to see any reason to move. The bed still smelled of her, and it made his head throb so hard his teeth hurt.

All right, he finally said to himself. She's gone. So what?

So everything. So he'd done it again, chased away somebody he loved. It was starting to look like that was his only real talent. The only thing he could do with people he loved: force them to run from him. What a rare and special gift.

He wallowed in his emotions for half an hour. Finally he sat up on the bed.

"Aw, the hell with it," he said. He didn't really believe it, but that didn't matter.

He had work to do.

It was still early on the Coast, but Arthur answered after six rings.

"It's R.J., Arthur," he said in a loud voice.

"I have my ears switched on, old chap. No need to bellow."

"Have you found anything yet?"

The old man gave a short bark of laughter. "You must remember how things work out here, laddy boy. As of my retirement seven years ago, I am capital N Nobody. It's going to take several weeks before my calls are returned."

"I remember," R.J. said. "I got another angle for you, if you're still willing to help."

"Of course I am, R.J. Of course I'll help."

"I have a composite picture, Arthur."

"You mean one of those dreadful drawings? My word, just like in the movies."

"This one isn't that bad. The guy has been recognized from the picture already."

"Well, send it to me, posthaste. I'll take it 'round and see what I can do."

"Thanks, Arthur. You'll have it tomorrow."

"Splendid."

"I don't know if this helps, Arthur, but there's a chance this guy had some training at one of the good drama schools."

"How so?"

"Well, I got a witness who says that's what his speech sounds like. Polished, like they teach actors."

"Used to teach, old boy. Used to teach. Nowadays oatmeal mouth is all the rage. But back then . . . Well, back then diction was one of the calling cards of a legitimate actor. That would mean either Carnegie or Juilliard, I should think."

"Juilliard? Here in Manhattan?"

"The same. And Carnegie in Pittsburgh. Now Carnegie-Mellon."

"Arthur, that's a real help."

"You mean I have provided a *lead*, my boy? How extraordinary. I'm delighted."

"I appreciate your help. I'll call when I find something."

"Godspeed, old chap. Godspeed."

R.J. hung up. The old boy would do his best, he thought with affection. Always had.

R.J.'s next call was to directory assistance in Pittsburgh. He got a number for the main switchboard at Carnegie-Mellon and called it.

R.J. got switched around several times until he had the Drama Department office. When he finally managed to get them to understand what he was after, he got disconnected. He called back and got the secretary again, who apologized and said she was still trying to figure out how the phones worked.

"I have the same problem with secretaries," R.J. told her.

She giggled, and R.J. heard her hit the switch.

She got it right this time. After three short buzzing rings, someone picked up the phone and R.J. spoke with a woman named Barbara who had a very nasal voice.

"I certainly don't advertise that I'm the senior faculty member," she said. "I may have to do something awful to Shirley for this."

"Who?"

"Shirley, the gal in the office. She could have given you the lighting teacher; he's been here almost as long. Of course, he probably wouldn't speak to you at all."

"Barbara, I'd like to ask your help in a murder investigation."

"If it takes time, forget it. We have three productions in the next month, and I'm doing a movie this spring."

"I just need you to look at a picture. Tell me if it's a former student."

"What makes you think he might be?"

"He has good speech."

She laughed, a funny, nasal little heh-heh-heh. "It would have to be quite a while back then," she said.

"It could be," R.J. told her.

"Well, send it along. I guess I can look at a picture."

———————◆———————

R.J. made a similar call to Juilliard. The only real difference was that he could drop the picture off in person, since the school was located in Manhattan.

He found the place easily enough, not too far from Lincoln Center, and located the office. He left the picture with a strange, pale young man who wore a pince-nez and bow tie.

R.J. felt reluctant to trust the picture to someone who looked like he belonged in a fish tank.

"You'll get this to the professor?" he asked.

The young man goggled damply at him. "I said I would."

"You won't forget or anything?"

The young man sighed. "At the moment I am keeping in memory, flawlessly, the entire keyboard oeuvre of J. S. Bach, Rachmaninoff, and Eric Satie. I think I can remember to hand an ugly picture to an old professor."

R.J. had to grin in spite of himself. "I guess maybe you can. But you should loosen up a little."

"How so?" the fish asked him, already bored.

"Learn some Jerry Lee Lewis oeuvre," R.J. said.

On his way back through midtown R.J. gradually lost the edge of excitement he'd been riding. He needed action, and dropping off a picture didn't do it for him.

The fight with Casey had hit him, even harder than he thought it had. Get a grip, he told himself. If it's over, it's over. It's happened to you before, it'll happen again.

He felt bad enough that he decided to stop off and see Hookshot on the way back to the office. Maybe his friend could coax a laugh out of him. Always had before.

But when R.J. came to the kiosk it was closed.

He blinked. Hookshot's place was never closed. Never. If he had to go someplace one of his urchins would watch the till.

Except it was closed now.

There was a raspy clatter behind him. R.J. whirled. Benny, the smart-ass kid, slid to a stop, popping his skateboard into the air and catching it casually.

"Yo, hey, you some kind of a friend of Hookshot's or something?"

R.J. looked at the kid. He looked worried—as worried as a snotty street punk could look.

"That's right. *Friend* is the right word. What about you?"

Benny pulled a black wad of fabric out of his battered backpack. "Yeah, funny. Lookit here." He held up the wad. R.J. took it, shook it out.

It was Hookshot's jacket.

R.J. looked at Benny. "Where'd you get this?"

"What, like I *stole* it? Fuck you."

"No, like where you'd get it? Hookshot wouldn't leave it lying around. He likes this jacket."

"No shit. Like I don't know that?"

R.J. threw a hand out. Benny was fast, but R.J. was faster, and he got a hand twisted into the kid's jacket. He lifted. The skateboard clattered to the sidewalk.

"Listen, Ace. I'd love to hang around and teach you some manners, but I think something's wrong with my friend. I need to know: Where—did—you—" he said, shaking the kid with each word, "get—this—jacket?"

"All right, shit! Give me fucking whiplash. I found it right here."

"Here? At the newsstand?"

"Yeah. What the fuck—" He stopped as R.J. shook him again. "Right here. It was stuck on the front there."

R.J. put Benny down. "What do you mean, 'stuck'?"

Benny snaked a hand in and out of his backpack. "With this." He held up an icepick, the handle wrapped with duct tape. "Fresh, huh?"

Hookshot lived in a tiny roach motel of an apartment on East 12th Street. He could have bought himself a brownstone on Fifth Ave or a co-op anywhere in the city, but he wanted to stay close to his roots. Either that or he was just cheap. A lot of millionaires were.

The building smelled like somebody had been boiling cabbage in dog piss. R.J. held his breath as he climbed the stairs to the apartment.

The up side to the place was that there was no doorman, no security of any kind. When nobody answered his knock, R.J. had no trouble kicking in the door.

He stood in the doorway looking for just a moment. "Shit," he said.

Hookshot was cheap, but he was neat. Always had been. He would not have left the place like this. The battered couch was flung on one end into the corner. Dishes and food were scattered across the floor. The curtains were ripped down.

It looked a lot like Casey's apartment had looked.

"Shit," R.J. said again. Heart pounding now as he

realized what that meant, he turned to go.

He stopped dead. So did his heart.

Skewered into the wall beside the door was a silver curve of metal.

Hookshot's hook.

Stunned, unwilling to believe what he was seeing, R.J. stepped closer. The hook was pinning something to the wall, a flimsy piece of sheer fabric. R.J. had seen it before, seen it recently. As he recognized it he stopped breathing, and everything went black for half a second.

It was a pair of Casey's panties.

CHAPTER 30

R.J. was down the stairs and out on the sidewalk in less than a minute. He sprinted up to the corner and flagged a cab. "Twenty bucks if you get me there in under ten minutes," he said, knowing it was impossible, knowing it didn't matter, it was too late, Casey was dead, Hookshot was dead, the killer was gone already.

"Get you *where* in ten minutes?" the cabbie asked.

R.J. froze. He had no idea *where*.

His brain whirled furiously. The killer was most likely holed up someplace safe, quiet, someplace R.J. could never find.

He realized he was panting and his palms were sweating. *Think, goddamn it.* But there was nothing to think about, no way to figure out where he had taken them.

Except . . .

R.J. knew the killer was really after him. Not Hookshot, not Casey—*him*. He'd known since the attempt on Casey. He didn't know how he knew it, but he knew it with certainty anyhow. He was the target.

That meant Casey and Hookshot were just the bait.

And bait had to be left in the open where it could be sniffed out.

Which meant the killer had taken them someplace that R.J. could find, *would* find—not right away, maybe not on the first try, but the killer wanted R.J. to find him eventually. Wanted to torture R.J. with a search, certainly, tantalize him with the knowledge of what was happening to Casey and Hookshot while he scrabbled around, hopelessly looking for them; he wanted it to drag on as long as possible.

But, ultimately, he wanted R.J. to find them.

He *wanted* to be found. He wanted to do whatever he did and he wanted to do it to R.J.

R.J. was as sure of that as he'd ever been of anything. The killer was out there someplace, waiting to be found.

But where? Not Casey's apartment; he had used it once already. Not the office, or he would have used some personal item of Wanda's.

Where?

"There's other people want the cab, mister," the cabbie said. "You want to go someplace or what?"

Someplace he would not expect, but a place that he would eventually have to come up with. Someplace—personal.

"Where to, buddy?" the cabbie said again.

R.J. blinked. Of course.

———————◆———————

It is going so beautifully. Just as he planned it; everything is perfect.

Now, though, he must simply wait. It isn't so hard, the waiting, not with everything in place. In the theater, one learns patience. He will practice it now. Waiting for his supporting player.

He will just check his props one last time, as he does before every performance.

Look at them, the two of them. His two little rabbits. Rabbits set to catch slightly bigger game.

The sight of them is deeply satisfying. Nodding quietly to himself, he reaches for his camera and takes a few more pictures. First the man, straining against his bonds, eyes blazing, thin muscles knotting with effort. Good. Wonderful. He could not have posed it better.

Now her. The woman. Oh, what a study she is. So much more interesting—much like the other woman, the mother. All cold fury and patience.

She is much tougher than he thought she would be. Perhaps there will be time to explore her, later, after the scene. It would make a fine epilogue to the larger drama.

It might be very fulfilling.

———————————————◆———————————————

The cabbie did not make it in under ten minutes. It was closer to fifteen by the time they pulled up in front of R.J.'s building.

R.J. paid him too much anyway. He leaped out of the car and flung the first bill out of his pocket, a twenty, at the front seat and sprinted into the building.

Just let me be on time, he prayed silently. He hadn't prayed for twenty years, but this seemed like a good time to start. Please, just let me be on time.

He went up the stairs without even noticing them. By the time he hit the landing of his floor he had his gun out and cocked.

He paused in front of his door and took a deep breath, steadied his gun hand.

One, two—

Smash!

He hit the door with everything he had, and it flew inward on its hinges, the lock a tattered thing.

R.J. flung himself through the doorway and stood at a crouch in the center of the room, gun ready. He looked to his left, to his right; in the kitchen. The bedroom. The closet.

Nothing.

Just to be certain, he stalked carefully into each room, letting the gun lead him, every sense quiveringly alert. But he knew it was no good.

The place was empty.

The killer was someplace else.

But where?

He sank onto the couch. He had been so sure this was the place. The killer was one jump ahead of him again. Had been the whole time. The guy seemed to know everything about him, what he was thinking, what he would do next.

So what would he do next? *Think,* damn it. Where else could he take them?

R.J. closed his eyes, rubbed his temples, tried to think like the killer. Where would he hole up?

Someplace quiet, someplace that R.J. would guess sooner or later, but not too soon. Someplace personal. But what could be more personal than his own apartment?

As it hit him, he was up and out the door before the thought really registered.

The shattered door flapped shut, open, half shut behind him.

He was already halfway down the stairs when the telephone rang. After three and a half rings the answering machine picked it up.

"Hello, R.J., it's Uncle Hank. I'm at your office. I came right over here because I got a complete profile for you, and it's a doozy.

"I think I know what the guy will do next, R.J. And it will happen soon. In the next day or two. So if you get this message, get ahold of Miss Wingate and *sit tight.* I think he will try to hit you through people close to you. I've sent your secretary out of town for the rest of the week, so she'll be okay.

"R.J., above all else, *don't* try to take this guy alone. When he's in his fugue state he'll be about five times as strong as you are. Please, son, be careful. *Tengas cuidado, hombre.*

"I'll see you soon."

———————————◆———————————

It was quicker this time getting across town. The cabbie had at first refused to go through Central Park. He'd changed his mind when R.J. held the gun to his head.

R.J. threw the guy another twenty, but he didn't look happy. That didn't seem too important.

Tony didn't open the door of the cab. That was a first, and it made R.J.'s pulse hammer even harder.

Nobody was there to open the front door of the building, either. R.J. went in fast, gun ready.

Tony was sound asleep in a chair over in the corner of the lobby. R.J. swore and ran for the elevator. Except—

Except that Tony was an ex-cop. The good kind. Tony would *never* sleep on the job. No matter what.

R.J. backtracked quickly and knelt beside the seated doorman, putting a finger to his throat.

He had a strong pulse. R.J. slapped his face.

Nothing. Then he noticed a very slight trickle of blood behind Tony's left ear.

R.J. took off the doorman's cap. Hidden by the hat, there was a welt above the ear the size of a Thanksgiving turkey. R.J. stood up.

The killer was here, upstairs, in his mother's apartment.

There could be no possible doubt.

She is teasing him, he is sure.

The way she just lies there. She refuses to squirm or plead with him. Difficult to plead, of course, with her mouth filled and taped shut. Still, she must feel helpless, naked and trussed like that.

The eyes are magnificent. She has not taken her eyes off him, not for a moment. She's hardly blinked.

And it is not fear with which she looks at him. It is simply a steady gaze. What strength; it gives him shivers. The possibilities of this woman! He must find time to get to know her. Absolutely must!

After. When he is done with the main event, her time will come.

Meanwhile . . .

He takes another picture.

R.J. did not take the elevator. He did not want the sound to alert the killer. And as hyped as he was now, he ran up the stairs as easily as if he was running downhill.

At the landing on his mother's floor he paused. It was one of the hardest things he'd ever done, but he forced himself to wait just a few seconds, to let his breath steady, to gain complete control.

He had to be like ice, to go in cold with every nerve steady and primed. If he let this guy get him rattled before the party even started, it was as good as over already.

A deep breath; let it out slowly. R.J. checked his gun one more time. The feel of it in his hand was a comfort, more than it had ever been before. Another deep breath; he drew back the hammer.

Moving as quickly and silently as he could, he went to the door.

R.J. listened at the door as hard as he could. He heard nothing. He hadn't really expected to. And he didn't need to. He was sure they were in there.

He braced himself across from the door.

One, two—

Smash!

He was into the small foyer, crouched, ready for anything—

And there was nothing. R.J. stood for a moment, his nostrils quivering, as if he could pick up the smell of the killer.

Which way?

Right down the hall—to the kitchen, the office?

No: R.J. knew how this guy was thinking. He would make it as personal as he could. And the most personal, insulting, maddening room would be—

His mother's bedroom.

Again following his gun barrel, R.J. slid down the hall. Past the closet, to the door of the bedroom. It was standing half open. R.J. let out a careful breath and eased up to it. He looked inside slowly.

Like some medieval painting of Hell, the scene in the bedroom assaulted him.

His mother had been proud of that massive headboard. It had been carved three hundred years ago. She'd brought it back from Italy and taken meticulous care of it. It had a beautifully made scene of Madonna and child carved into it.

And right now it had Hookshot tied to the top like a gargoyle.

He was wearing only his boxer shorts. His wrists and feet were tied behind his back and then looped over the point at the top center of the headboard, so he hung out over the top of the bed.

His eyes bulged out and all the veins in his face and neck were knotted and standing out like the ropes that bound him. And as he saw R.J. peer cautiously into the room, he frantically swung his eyes around, trying to draw R.J.'s attention to something. But R.J. was not looking at Hookshot any longer.

Beneath Hookshot lay Casey.

She was completely naked, tied up like a Christmas goose. Her hands were tied to the headboard and her ankles bound together. A piece of duct tape covered her mouth, but her eyes were clear. Frightened, yes, but not panicked, not shattered. She looked back at him with cool intelligence.

Around her head, spread out like a hand of cards, were half a dozen Polaroid pictures.

For a moment R.J. forgot everything: forgot where he was and what he was doing and why he was there with the gun in his hand.

All he could see was Casey.

His woman.

The fight was forgotten now. Someone had done this to *his woman*.

The same somebody had killed his mother. Hurt his friend. Flattened his childhood bicycle, haunted his dreams, tried to kill him, given him this scar on his chin.

"And here I am," said a voice as soft and cold as a snowflake.

Before R.J. could whirl and fire, a very sharp steel point appeared at his throat and pushed lightly, just hard enough to break the skin and get the message across.

"Wonderful entrance," the voice said. "Just perfect. But I'll take that now."

And the man plucked the gun away as if R.J. was as weak as a child.

CHAPTER 31

R.J. turned slowly, his hands up at shoulder level. A hundred thoughts fought for control of his mind, but they all vanished down the drain when he finished his turn and saw who was holding the point to his neck.

It was him.

The Scary Guy.

That same bland face, with the deep, twisted eyes. Those eyes that had stared out at him from his dreams all those long years ago. Except for the eyes, a completely uninteresting face.

The right hand was more interesting than the face. It held a sword. A fencing foil with the tip sharpened to what R.J. could feel was a very keen point. A point that had zeroed in on his throat and not wavered since it drew first blood.

R.J. looked up along the blade and into those cold, inhuman eyes. They seemed to draw him onward, almost as if some private part of him were falling into them, falling down, down . . .

"Yes," said the killer. "You feel it too, don't you? We are already connected."

"We're connected by your pigsticker, anyway," R.J. said. "You mind moving it off my Adam's apple?"

"Connected by a great deal more and you know it. Don't be shy about this," the monster said, but he moved the point back a half inch.

"Thanks," R.J. said.

"I have waited an awfully long time for this. Permit me to introduce myself." He said it with his hard-edged, practiced diction, like someone on a stage trying to reach the back rows. He thinks he's acting, R.J. thought.

"My name is John Dexter." The killer made a bow and gave a flourish with the sword, ending with a small stab at R.J.'s chest that left a scratch and then withdrew.

"I think you can ease up on the connection bit there, John," R.J. said, flinching back from the sword's point.

"Ah, but our connection is the whole *point*—of our meeting," Dexter said, stabbing again to underline his pun.

Jesus, I have to get a homicidal maniac who thinks he's funny, R.J. thought.

"To begin with, we have this unfinished piece of theater between us." Dexter moved the sword's tip forward and poked at R.J.'s arm. R.J. could feel it puncture his bicep.

"Sorry if I don't share your enthusiasm for murder as an art form," R.J. said.

"And of course, we have both lost our mothers. That's quite a bond, isn't it?" He stabbed lightly again, at R.J.'s other arm this time.

What with the sight of Casey and Hookshot bound to his mother's bed, and the sure knowledge that this was the man that had killed his mother, and the series of small wounds with the sword tip, it was all R.J. could do to stop himself from jumping at the guy and the hell with the consequences.

But he made himself stay calm. If he could draw out the killer, keep him from doing anything for a while, that was all to the good. The longer this went on, the better chance he would have to find an opening.

And he would find an opening. Maybe not a perfect one, but that didn't matter. All that mattered was closing his fingers around Dexter's throat and squeezing. And that would happen. It had to happen. Even if it happened with the sword point in his gut. That didn't matter either.

So he played the game. "I wouldn't think you had a mother, sport," R.J. said.

"Oh, yes," Dexter said, with a small stab at R.J.'s thigh. "Not a *movie star,* of course. But a mother for all that. And a good one, while she lasted." He smiled, a pale and alien smile.

"You kill her too?"

The eyes grew impossibly dark and deep. It seemed to R.J. that the pupils were actually whirling, sucking him in like a vortex.

"Of course I did," Dexter said softly. R.J. seemed to hear him from a great distance. "I learned very early about my special talent. Talent will out, you know.

"Mine 'outed' on a series of neighborhood pets. Pets always seem more important to people in trailer parks, have you noticed?" And he whipped the tip across R.J.'s forehead. "We weren't all born into mansions, you know."

"And we didn't all grow up strangling poodles," R.J.

said. The sharp pain had snapped the sense of falling into Dexter's eyes, and now he felt the blood starting on his forehead, a slow trickle across his brow.

Dexter didn't seem to notice. He went right on with his monologue. "The neighbors began to suspect it was me." He smiled shyly, like a kid. R.J. thought the sight of that innocent smile was the scariest thing he'd seen yet. "I was just a boy. Still learning caution, you see? Because the wonder of it, the beautiful ache of taking those precious little lives—it was so overwhelming I couldn't believe no one else felt it. I couldn't fully believe it was something I had to hide.

"Some busybody told my parents. And the walls in those trailers are thin. I heard my mother and father discussing what to do about Young John being so *different.*"

He laughed. "Well"—he fluttered the sword in a modest wave—"it was really only one small step from Pekingese to parent, wasn't it? I can't take much credit for the deed. It was primitive, clumsy. But the scene after—Ah, that showed promise. Poor young lad, orphaned in a tragic fire. So young, so all alone."

"Jesus," said R.J. "You really enjoyed that, huh?"

The eyes looked at him, through him, beyond him.

"Enjoy is an inadequate concept," he said. "I was—fulfilled. Transformed. Transmuted from the base clay of a trailer park into the lofty stuff beyond dreams. I became something other, something different. Better."

"Better?" R.J. goaded. "You mean you moved up to strangling Dobermans?"

The eyes locked on his, and it occurred to R.J. that he hadn't seen them blink. "Goading me is a rather obvious tactic, and it won't work," Dexter said. "You and I have a single, immutable destiny to fulfill, and you cannot change it. Even I could not change it. I know that now. We will have to find a way to make you accept it too," he said and stabbed, deeper this time, into R.J.'s left arm.

This time R.J. could not stop himself from hissing with the pain. He looked up to see the eyes still on him.

"Good." Dexter nodded. "You see? If I give you just enough pain you will start to believe it too. You will have to."

R.J. breathed deeply. The shock of the numerous small stab wounds was starting to make him weak. He knew that if he didn't do something soon, it would be too late.

"All right," he said, "so it wasn't Dobermans. A guy of your caliber probably went right to Shetland ponies."

Dexter smiled. "As a matter of fact, I fought for many years to stop myself altogether. I thought it was wrong. A few times a year I would be flooded by these glorious feelings and tear myself apart with guilt. That is how I found acting. I discovered that the right part was a substitute for what I needed. Oh, a very poor substitute, to be sure, but it worked. And as my career began, I became *normal* for a while.

"And then I met your mother."

For the first time real emotion showed on that bland face and it became a monster mask, a disguise to frighten children.

"Your mother. Belle Fontaine. Queen of the screen. Idol of millions. How I worshiped her. Oh, how I believed that being admitted into her mere presence meant I had arrived, had finally climbed the pinnacle of professional recognition! It was to have been my great break—an audition for Belle Fontaine!"

In spite of himself, R.J. was impressed. Dexter was good: He made the words ring, made it all seem magical.

"And I was ushered into that glorious presence. And your mother took one glance at me and said, in her beautiful, resonant voice, the velvet voice I loved so much—she said, 'Get that drab little creep out of here.'"

He paused. Even his silence was filled with theatrical tension.

"'Get that drab little creep out of here,'" he repeated, very softly now. "A death sentence. Delivered in that wonderful voice."

Dexter whirled, transformed into a fountain of amazed energy.

"She meant *ME!*" he said, in a voice like a pipe organ, and R.J. felt the hair rise on the back of his neck. "She was talking about *me,* calling me a drab little creep!" And then softer again, pleading, "There had to be some mistake. Perhaps she was having a bad day. Maybe I reminded her of someone else—but I could look different, I would show her, I was not drab. I was *neutral*—I could be *anyone.* If she could see—if she would just see . . ."

It was a wonderful moment of hope. R.J. had never seen it done better, not in any movie or play. This was a great performance. If only he could live through it.

Dexter went on very quietly. "I tried, you know. I followed her for two weeks. I became a dozen different people, two dozen. She would have to notice me sooner or later, to recognize my talent. She would *have* to.

"But—she—*did not.*"

"I did," R.J. said, and the eyes came back to him with a click he could almost feel. "I noticed."

"Yes," he said. "You did. You noticed. A boy. *Her* boy. You see, right away there was the beginning of this bond between us, though you still deny the idea. You noticed me."

"I knew it was the same person, but you were in all these different disguises," R.J. said. "I thought I was nuts. Then I figured you must be. I was right."

"You'd like to think so, wouldn't you? You'd like it to be that simple, to remove any blame from your dear departed mother. But the facts are never so simple. The truth is not a tame animal. The fact is, you noticed me. No one else did. And now after all those years we are together again. Because there is something between us, and it is unfinished and can only be completed in one way.

"With your death."

CHAPTER 32

R.J.?" Henry Portillo called softly. He stood cautiously at the shattered door of R.J.'s apartment. He held his gun out, ready.

There was a small sound. Portillo let his breath out halfway, and with a fluid grace gained by years of practice, he slid through the door in a shooter's crouch.

Nothing. Then he heard the small sound again. Portillo moved carefully across the room toward the closet.

He whipped the closet door open and stood back and to the side, his gun covering the interior of the closet.

"On the floor, now!" he commanded.

"Jesus, man, please don't kill me!" a voice said.

Portillo saw only a pair of battered high-top basketball shoes under baggy green pants.

"Come out slow and easy and I let you live," Portillo said. "Fuck with me and I'm gonna cool you."

"All right, no problem, be easy, my man," said the voice.

A kid of about sixteen came out, hands high. He had a slight mustache and wore a striped shirt.

"I'm here, man, no problems, okay?"

"What's your name, *chico*?" Henry asked him.

"Ronnie."

Portillo gestured with the gun. "On the floor, Ronnie, facedown."

The kid scrambled down onto his face. "Whatever you say, man."

Portillo patted him down and took a wicked-looking black device that said NINJA NIFE on the handle.

He also pulled out a few handfuls of portable valuables belonging to R.J.: some cufflinks, a hammered silver-and-turquoise belt buckle Portillo had given him, a pair of Argyle socks.

Portillo snorted. "What are the socks for, *chico*?"

"I liked 'em. Never seen socks like that."

Portillo stood over the kid. "All right, Ronnie. Slow and easy, show me your hands and sit up."

Ronnie did as he was told.

"What're you doing here, Ronnie?"

Ronnie shrugged. "Just, you know. I seen the door like that and thought, you know. Get some stuff."

"You see what happened to the door?"

"No man, I swear, it was like that. That's why I come in here. Look, I won't do it again—"

Portillo stepped closer. "Don't fuck with me! I want the truth!"

"That is the truth, I swear to Jesus! Please, man, honest!" The kid almost foamed at the mouth he was so scared. Portillo believed him.

"Stand up, Ron." The kid did so and Portillo got up into his face, staring him down with his best hard cop glare. "Listen good, Ron." He pulled the hammer back on his gun; it was very loud. He put the barrel right up to the kid's face.

"This what you want, *chico*?"

"Please, man, no." The kid was shaking.

"I want you to remember something Ron. Next time you think about getting some stuff. Or doing some drugs. Look right down there, Ron. See the bullet?"

"I see it, please—"

"That bullet has your name on it, *chico*. Remember it, 'cause it's gonna remember you."

Portillo held the gun where it was for just a moment longer. Then he turned the kid around, booted him in the ass, and told him, "Get outta here and don't come back."

Ron was long gone by the time Portillo eased the hammer down and holstered his gun.

And now what? he thought, suddenly bone-tired beyond what he should have been.

He tried to shake off the fatigue, but it wasn't working. Because the broken door meant only one thing to Henry Portillo.

The killer had R.J.

CHAPTER 33

R.J. looked into the mad eyes and beyond them, to Casey and Hookshot. "As a matter of fact," R.J. said, "your death would wrap things up a lot better for me."

The smile was almost warm, but with the terror of those eyes it was mad, completely crazy. "Of course. You have to think so. That completes your character arc; it's your motivation. And you will get your chance, don't fret. But theater is a tension of opposites. There must be conflict."

Without taking his eyes off him, Dexter stepped back, picked up a Polaroid camera, and took two quick shots of R.J. before dropping it on the bed again. He grabbed at a large gym bag lying beside the bed.

"All great theatrical moments contain a balanced tension of sex"—he whipped his blade backward and caressed Casey's bare stomach with the sword's tip as he unzipped the bag, his eyes never blinking—"and death."

R.J. looked up from the thin line of red the sword left on Casey's stomach. Her eyes were shouting at him, *Kill him, R.J.* He tried to tell her with his eyes, *I will.*

Slowly, Dexter pulled something from the bag and held it up for R.J. to see. R.J. snapped his focus back, away from Casey. His breath puffed out in surprise when he saw what the maniac held out.

It was a plastic sword, a kid's toy. A foot and a half long, with a broad, lime-green blade.

Dexter flipped it to R.J., who caught it reflexively by its cheap gold handle. "Defend yourself," Dexter told him.

Think, Henry. Think.

But he couldn't think. Since this whole business had begun he'd felt numb, brain-fogged, one foot in the grave.

Come on, *viejo.* You have the killer's profile. You have the smarts in that old head somewhere. Where has he taken R.J.?

He closed his eyes, so weary, and let his mind roam. Nothing came to him. Nothing but images of his life stretching back so many years to the dust of the high desert. His work.

Belle.

I'm sorry, Belle. I just don't have it anymore.

So damned tired. But he had to try to find them, even if he was only going through the motions. He was trapped by his sense of duty and honor, by his feelings for R.J.—and by thirty years of loving Belle, though she had never given him the slightest sign that she loved him too. He had never kissed her, except on the cheek. Never touched more than her hand. Never even seen the inside of her bedroom—

Henry Portillo's eyes snapped open.

R.J. looked down at the plastic sword in his hand. It was a foot and a half long and felt sturdy—for a kid's toy. But as his only hope, against a crazy man?

He had a rugged toy and half a dozen small holes in him. He faced a powerful, incredibly fast maniac with a sword.

R.J. looked up at Dexter. He expected to see a sneer, a mocking grin, a sardonic smile. But Dexter looked completely serious. "Is this your idea of conflict?"

"You're supposed to lose," the maniac said. "You *have* to lose. Audiences want to see Me overcome adversity and gain just revenge for the wrongs inflicted on Me. But *you* gain sympathy, even glory, by your hopeless struggle."

"Jesus Christ."

"Yes. It's a marvelous theatrical moment, isn't it? All the great tragedies have this sort of thing."

Dexter swished the sword, casually flicking a rip in R.J.'s shirt. "Shakespeare is wonderful at this sort of thing. Macbeth, Brutus, even Iago—all gain a nobility in their deaths they can never attain in life. Just as you will."

R.J. stared at Dexter's face. It seemed to shift as he spoke, flowing from one set to another to fit his words.

He's completely whacked out, R.J. thought. He doesn't even know who he is.

R.J. shook his head slowly. It didn't matter. He could be facing all ten of Dexter's multiple personalities, all at the same time, and it wouldn't matter.

Because R.J. felt a tide rising inside him. It was part despair and part rage, and it centered on one thought. If this was the only chance he was going to get, then so be it. It was a long shot—so long it was off the board—but it was better than no shot at all.

He was going to go for it, beat this psycho with his teeth and nails if he had to. Dexter had been tormenting him, deliberately doing all he could to drive him slowly crazy. But one thing he maybe hadn't counted on.

It had worked.

R.J. was more than a little nuts himself right now. And he would crawl naked through burning broken glass to get his hands around Dexter's throat.

Dexter had shoved him into a corner where he had only one option. R.J. was going to take it.

He waved the little toy sword. It had a thick, hollow plastic blade, about two inches wide. It would help to block some of the sword thrusts. And then, if he could get close . . .

A foil is only dangerous at the tip. It kills by stabbing. It has no edge at all. The blade is maybe three feet long from handle to tip.

The swordsman needs at least three feet of distance from his target, plus a little maneuvering room. So if R.J. could get inside that three-foot arc, the foil would be useless.

That was the theory, anyway.

Dexter made a smooth lunge at R.J., so fast it was almost invisible. Before R.J. could react Dexter was away again, and a small red flower blossomed on R.J.'s left hand.

"Have at you," Dexter said.

R.J. flexed his hand. It still worked, but it stung like hell. He stared at the other man, now looking like a coiled snake in his ready position: left hand on his hip, knees bent, deadly sharp tip pointed right at R.J.

"Ha!" Dexter said. He stamped his foot and extended the tip with terrible speed. R.J. blundered away to the side, almost tripping over his own feet. He caught himself and stood erect again, but not before he felt a searing pain in his calf muscle. Dexter had pricked him again.

"First blood," said Dexter. His face was a grinning mask, looking like Cyrano and the Three Musketeers and all the noble heroes with swords.

R.J. shook his head; the man's face kept shifting, flowing from one role to another. It was as unnerving as the stab wounds.

"First doesn't matter," said R.J. "Only last counts."

"Well said," said Dexter, and then his face shifted again and he lunged.

R.J.'s arms were already stiff where he had been stabbed. He felt blood running into his eyes from the scratch on his forehead, and his legs were leaden. With every bit of energy and speed he could muster, he just barely beat aside the point of Dexter's sword. Before he could do any more than stagger to the side, Dexter had danced away.

"Bravo," Dexter said. He was not even breathing hard.

R.J. recovered into a crouch, the pathetic toy sword held out. He drew his left arm across his forehead. It came away wet with sweat and blood. He could feel his lips pulling back into a snarl.

Dexter came again. A graceful swish, faster than a snake striking. The lunge was aimed right for his eye. R.J. clumsily batted the point away again, just managing not to stumble to his knees as he tried to move sideways.

It was closer this time, and the tip ran through his shirt and raised a welt along his shoulder.

And even closer with the next lunge. Dexter came right at him again without pausing, and R.J., whirling to the side, felt a red-hot pain along his cheek.

R.J. grunted involuntarily with the sting of Dexter's blade. He jumped back, raising a hand to his cheek. It had missed his eye by about an inch and a half.

He was not going to make it. Dexter was too fast, too revved up, and he was getting stronger and faster while R.J. got slower and weaker.

The odds were just too long. He was going to die here.

R.J. had moved in a full circle in his clumsy attempts to stay away from the point of Dexter's foil. He was now once again facing Casey on the bed. And as his gaze fell on her, she made frantic signals with her eyes.

R.J. stared, and as he did Dexter came again.

Because he had been distracted he was half a second slow and barely managed to get his arm up in an instinctive cover-up move. The point was aimed at his throat. It found his arm instead.

"Aahh!" R.J. cried involuntarily as the point plowed into his left bicep. He could feel the tissue of his muscle clinging to the steel blade as Dexter pulled it out and quickly stepped back again.

In spite of the pain, in spite of the fact that his first look had nearly allowed Dexter to skewer him, R.J. looked at Casey again.

She was waggling her eyebrows frantically. In other circumstances it would have looked comical.

He shook his head slightly; it didn't make any sense.

She rolled her eyes downward, toward her feet. And as he watched, Casey lifted her feet slightly, showing him that they were tied together but not tied down.

And then Dexter was at him again. R.J. beat aside the point and stepped to the side, trying to keep an eye on Casey for another clue. What could she be trying to say that was so important? He was fighting for his life and hers—and losing. What could she possibly have to tell him that—

Her feet. They were not tied down. She could move her feet.

Move them in a kick, for instance.

R.J. swore, wiping the blood and sweat from his eyes. If he could maneuver Dexter just right, with Casey's help he'd have him off-balance. And then . . .

Dexter lunged again. R.J. batted at the point furiously and stepped to the side. The sword still plowed a furrow along his forearm.

This was no good. If he waited to react to Dexter, he'd be shish-kabobed in two more minutes. He had to be proactive about this, move Dexter into a position where Casey could help. But as he gathered himself for his own lunge, Dexter made a rapid series of passes with the foil.

R.J. ducked the first, batted away the second, and felt the third slip into his thigh with shocking pain. As Dexter ripped out the point, R.J. knew he could not stand too many more wounds like that one.

If he was going to survive, and have any chance at all to take Dexter out, it had to be now.

R.J. circled to his right, away from the point of Dexter's sword. He was limping heavily, and everything hurt like hell.

"You have fought well, my friend," Dexter said, and his face became heroic. "But your cause is hopeless. And so I must—"

R.J. had heard enough. He knew enough about theater to know that there was never any action during the hero's monologue. The hero—and Dexter thought of himself as the hero—had to have his say, for as long as he felt like saying it.

This was his chance.

R.J. jumped. With all his strength he swung the plastic sword at the foil, knocking it to one side. But before he could bring his hands back again Dexter had stepped smoothly to the side.

He stopped two feet from the edge of the bed, two feet from Casey's reach.

"Well done," Dexter said. "You have—"

R.J. jumped again. This time Dexter saw it coming and stepped to his left. Into position.

"I'm sorry, my friend," he said. "But you—"

And Casey swung her feet. Every muscle in her body stood out with the effort as she planted the point of her two big toes squarely in the back of Dexter's legs.

Dexter buckled.

R.J. jumped at him.

Dexter's reactions were faster than anything R.J. had ever seen before. As his knees gave way from Casey's kick and he went backward, he still managed to bring the point up and hold it out toward R.J. as he fell back onto the bed.

R.J. could not stop his leap. If he could have, he wouldn't have. He knew this was the only chance he was going to get. Holding the stupid little plastic sword in front of him he continued his dive onto the falling killer.

R.J. saw the point of the foil come up and managed to twist aside slightly. But it still took him through the shoulder, and he felt it pierce him and poke out through the back of his shirt. The pain was worse than anything else he could remember. It was a live, red-hot thing chewing at him, and time slowed down as the whole world refocused around that pain.

But then there was the hard, slow-motion impact as he crashed into Dexter. The plastic sword smacked into Dexter's sword arm with the full weight of R.J.'s body behind it. Dexter's hand fell away from the grip, and for a moment he lay stunned and unmoving.

In that moment R.J. closed his fingers around Dexter's throat.

It felt better than sex, drugs, or booze. It was the purest, cleanest, wildest, most satisfying thrill R.J. had ever felt. He forgot about the sword sticking out from his shoulder. He forgot about Casey, still flailing her gorgeous naked legs at Dexter's head. He forgot about his mother, his son, his whole life, as the feeling of his fingers squeezing on Dexter's throat became everything there was and he wanted it to go on forever.

R.J. squeezed. He didn't feel Dexter's increasingly ineffective blows hitting him. He didn't notice when the blows slowed, then stopped.

He didn't even see Dexter's face turn red, then blue, and finally almost black, his tongue hanging out. All he saw were those pale, unblinking, emotionless, bottomless gray eyes, and the eyes made R.J. squeeze on, harder and harder.

He knew he was getting weaker as he lost more blood from his shoulder. Things started to go dim, and he didn't hear the terrible small crunching sounds from Dexter's throat, didn't see that Casey's thrashing was a different kind now as she tried to get him to stop squeezing the lifeless husk of John Dexter.

Just before he passed out, R.J. thought he heard something, at last.

It was a voice, calling out, "Police! Freeze!"

It sounded a lot like Henry Portillo.

CHAPTER 34

They kept R.J. overnight in the hospital. The emergency-room doctor, a young guy with pimples and red hair, made a lot of jokes about pincushions. R.J. didn't laugh.

But when he was lying in bed later, he smiled a lot. It might have been the painkillers kicking in. The feeling of relief from all those stab wounds was enough to bring a smile to the face of a gargoyle.

And then, maybe it wasn't just the painkillers. It might have been the visitors.

Hookshot came by. They'd refitted his hook, and he was even wearing his black silk jacket.

R.J. looked at him fondly. "How in the hell did you get that jacket back so fast?"

"Benny brought it by." Hookshot laughed. "Kid's got a heart under all that mean. Lookit here!" He held up the sleeve and the tail of the jacket to show where the ice pick had pierced them. The holes were neatly mended. "Benny took it over to Mendlebaum, got it patched."

"Nice kid," R.J. said, drifting a little from the drugs.

"Bullshit," said Hookshot. He took a slip of paper from the jacket's pocket. "Gave me the goddamn bill."

R.J. smiled, and he came as close to laughing as he could with all those damned tubes going in and out of him.

"Anyway," Hookshot said at last, "I'll leave you folks be. You mend up, brother." He snapped a half-salute with his gleaming silver hook and was gone.

R.J. reached out to the side of the bed. A hand met and held his, and he looked up into Casey's eyes.

Casey had stayed with him in the ambulance the whole way to the hospital, right beside him, not letting the paramedics bully her out of the way. Uncle Hank had been along for the ride too, flashing his badge when they tried to put him off the ambulance. But Portillo had finally left when they got R.J. patched up and into a bed. He'd said he was going to get the door fixed at R.J.'s apartment and camp out there.

Casey stayed. And all through the night, as R.J. drifted in and out of a lightly drugged sleep, Casey was there beside the bed, watching him, even holding his hand.

In the morning, before he was released, R.J. had three more visitors.

He had just finished his breakfast when he heard hard shoes in the hall. They were cop shoes, no question. For some reason cop shoes always sound different. The cop might be wearing the same shoes as anyone else, but they had a sound all their own. It was a little harder, a little brisker.

And sure enough, the sound paused at his door and Lieutenant Kates came in, followed by Bertelli and

Boggs. At the door, Kates turned to Boggs and said, "Wait in the hall."

R.J. grinned. He could see Boggs hated that, hated it like hell, but he shut up and did what he was told. R.J. knew it was the only apology he was going to get from Kates. It was enough.

Bertelli, standing behind Kates, gave him a quick grin and a thumbs-up.

"Well, Brooks," Kates said, looking at him with faint distaste. "Pretty close to a major fuckup. Pardon my language, Miss Wingate."

"Don't give it another fucking thought, Lieutenant," she said sweetly.

Kates took a breath, then heard what she'd said and turned to look at her. But Casey looked innocently back and Kates was obviously not sure he'd heard it. He cleared his throat and looked at Bertelli, who was trying not to laugh, and then at R.J., who smiled at him.

"Go on, Fred," R.J. said. "What were you saying?"

But Kates was blushing. In the end, he could only stammer out a few vague statements encouraging R.J. to be more cooperative in the future.

R.J. was glad to agree. For the first time in weeks, he believed there was going to be a future.

Kates left, dragging Boggs with him. Bertelli hung behind just long enough to shake his head at R.J. and Casey and tell them, very softly, "shame on youse." Then he was gone too, his cop shoes clicking after the others.

"You talk to your mother with that mouth?" R.J. asked Casey.

She snorted. "You should hear what my mother says back."

They got back to his apartment a little bit after noon. R.J. was surprised at how weak he felt. But as the doctor reminded him when he checked out, he had lost a lot of blood and would need to take it easy for a few days.

R.J. didn't need the reminder. With the sling and the dozen or so bandages hanging from his body he felt like a medical experiment gone bad.

Uncle Hank was waiting for them at the apartment, and true to his word, he had managed to get the door fixed. R.J. paused to admire the new door. Uncle Hank stood beside him.

"Steel-reinforced," he said, rapping on the door with his knuckle. "I had them put in steel around the frame, with six-inch bolts to hold it in. And two new deadbolts, top and bottom." With a small flourish, he handed the new keys to R.J.

"For Christ's sake, Uncle Hank. What in hell did you think I keep in here?"

The older man looked slightly hurt, but he smiled through it. "You, *chico*. You keep *you* in here."

There was nothing much to say to that. So R.J. leaned on Hank's arm and let him help him through the door.

"Sit," Portillo told him. "Just sit. You need to eat something."

"What are you thinking about feeding him?" Casey asked with a raised eyebrow. "The doctor gave strict orders—"

Portillo cut her off. "I have been dealing with wounded men my whole life. I know what to feed him."

"Nothing greasy or spicy, not for at least three days."

"Is *that* what you think about Mexican cooking? Because—"

R.J. raised his voice as much as he could and butted in. "Guys? Can you get me to the chair and *then* kill each other?"

Casey took one elbow and Henry the other, and he managed to sink weakly into the easy chair, beside a frantically blinking answering machine. He sat for a moment with his eyes closed and then reached over and played back the messages. He could hear Casey and Portillo fussing around together in the kitchen.

Probably arguing about what sort of gruel I can have, he thought with a very feeble smile.

He rolled the message tape.

The first call was from Pittsburgh. The nasal voice identified herself as Barbara, the drama professor he'd spoken to at Carnegie-Mellon. She said she'd gotten the picture and was pretty sure it was a former student, John Dexter.

R.J. snorted.

The next was from Arthur in Hollywood. He said he'd had a bit of luck and thought he'd found someone to identify the picture. It looked rather like a chap named Dexter, quite a good actor, really.

The last message was from Wanda, in Buffalo, telling him that if he let anything happen to him she was going to kick his ass.

He lay back in the chair, his head lolling on the headrest. It was all too much, had finished up too quickly, and he felt like he hadn't caught up with himself yet.

The voices in the kitchen heated up a little and then died away. R.J., feeling happy for a change, drifted off to sleep.

Much later that night, after Hank had gone to the air-
port to catch the shuttle back to Quantico, R.J. lay in
bed, his eyes closed, still sorting through all that had
happened.

He felt a gentle feather of a touch on his cheek and
opened his eyes.

Casey stood beside the bed, looking down at him.

"How do you feel?"

"Okay. A little bit weak, but not so bad."

She sat on the edge of the bed beside him and for a
few minutes they were silent.

"You're all right, Wingate," R.J. said.

"You better believe it," she said.

He took her hand again and held it for a moment.

"Thanks, Casey," he said after a while.

"For what?"

"For staying with me. I—it means a lot to me."

"Forget it," she scoffed. "This pays for itself. This is
a great finish for my story."

He turned his head to look at her full for a minute,
then smiled.

"You know what, Wingate?"

"What?"

"You're full of shit."

She finally smiled, softly, almost tenderly, looking
into his eyes. Then she leaned all the way over and
kissed him softly on the lips.

"Maybe," she said.

Available by mail from